The Road Back *to* Sweetgrass

The Road Back to
Sweetgrass

A NOVEL

Linda LeGarde Grover

UNIVERSITY OF MINNESOTA PRESS

Minneapolis

London

"Margie-enjiss" and "Animoosh" were published as the two-part story "The Rice Pickers" in *Fiction on a Stick: Stories by Writers from Minnesota*, edited by Daniel Slager (Minneapolis: Milkweed Editions, 2008).

An excerpt from "The Art of Dressing a Rabbit" was originally published in *Duluth Budgeteer News*, June 14, 2009.

Published by the University of Minnesota Press
111 Third Avenue South, Suite 290
Minneapolis, MN 55401-2520
http://www.upress.umn.edu

LIBRARY OF CONGRESS CATALOGING-IN-PUBLICATION DATA
Grover, Linda LeGarde.
The road back to Sweetgrass / Linda LeGarde Grover.
ISBN 978-0-8166-9269-9 (hc) | 978-0-8166-9916-2 (pb)
1. Indian women—North America—Fiction. 2. Indians of North America—Social conditions—Fiction. 3. Ojibwe Indians—Fiction. 4. Minnesota—Fiction. I. Title.
PS3607.R6777R63 2014
813'.6—dc23
                                                            2014003133

Printed in the United States of America on acid-free paper

The University of Minnesota is an equal-opportunity educator and employer.

24 23 22   10 9 8 7 6

To my dad, Jerry LeGarde

Contents

The Odissimaa Bag

TODAY, THE OPENING DAY *of the Mozhay Point Ojibwe Reservation's wild rice harvest, cumulus clouds drift slowly over the boat landing on Lost Lake, bringing with them the scent of sweetgrass. Among the ricers who pause to inhale the blessing are a teenage boy and his father who park at the side of the road in a gray-primered Ford truck faded to the near no-color of glass, a young married couple who argue as they carry her parents' canoe toward the water, and an elderly woman who has just placed a pot of coffee to boil on an old car grill over a campfire.*

On this western end of Mozhay it happens that way occasionally when the wind comes from the northeast, the scent of sweetgrass edging and swirling from the LaForce family allotment land, its source somewhere near the maple sugarbush, making its invisible way past the cabin and down the driveway to the road, where it dissipates and fades when it reaches the boat landing. The Mozhay Point ricers, who know that no sweetgrass grows on the LaForce land, even in the swamp on the far side of the allotment, occasionally stop in their work to wonder about this; the scent reminds us that we have been blessed by the Creator in all ways, understood or otherwise, here during our time on Mother Earth, and so we accept the mystery for what it is.

Yet in the old Muskrat family sugarbush, there near the middle of the land that more than a century ago became the LaForce family land allotment, is where spirits tread so lightly that their feet, transparent as the air, make no more mark on the ground than air itself; with every step the scent, invisibly compressed and released, renews and rises into the LaForce allotment atmosphere.

Below the earth that is covered by leaves in fall, snow in winter, mud in spring, and sparse northern moss in summer, a small deerskin bag sewn with red thread and blue beads holds an infant's umbilical cord, an odissimaa, wrapped in dried sweetgrass.

Bezhig: The Frybread Makers

The Power of Frybread

2014

AS SHE APPROACHED ELDERHOOD, Margie Robineau had come to be regarded as unarguably the hands-down best frybread maker on the entire Mozhay Point Indian Reservation. Although she had unofficially held that title since she was twenty-two, Indian Country protocol and etiquette called for no recognition beyond "that Margie, she makes pretty good frybread" until after Annie Buck, venerable elder and longtime frybread queen, had died. Only then, and after a decent and respectful interval, did Margie become the person to ask about the fine points of frybread making: baking soda, powder, or yeast; commodity flour or Gold Medal; lard or Crisco, shortening or oil; spoon or hands. Granulated sugar or powdered, rolled or sprinkled. Cinnamon. Honey. Jelly. Butter (no inquiries about margarine). Maple syrup. Loaded Indian tacos or frybread plain and simple.

Margie's frybread was so light it all but rose from the plate, so tender as to be all but unfelt in the mouth, so tasty that the very thought that the moment couldn't last forever brought to the eater an undertone of sorrow that added an intangible brine, like a grain of salt from dried tears yet to be wept. The golden rings that bloomed as they deep-fried in hot lard grew from a dough mixture that she varied from day to day: sometimes she used wheat flour, sometimes white; sometimes she added blueberries. On occasion, if she was in a hurry, she didn't even let the dough rest before she fried it, sending it into the near-smoking grease deprived of its gestation in the dark and quiet of the dishcloth-covered mixing bowl. Variations didn't seem to matter: the resulting quality was always the same.

She never minded if someone wanted to observe her while she cooked. After all, wasn't that the way of old-time Ojibwe tradition, to share, to teach by example, to learn by watching? Many watched, committing to memory her actions: they noted that she used sometimes her hands, sometimes a metal measuring cup for the flour; sometimes her hands, sometimes a tablespoon from the silverware drawer for the leavening; sometimes her hands, sometimes a wooden spoon to stir. Those combinations, along with the precisely inexact points at which she added warm water, were tried by women all over Mozhay Point. Why, then, they asked themselves and each other, could no one else duplicate the frybread that Margie made in her tiny, dark, and crowded kitchen at home in the Sweetgrass cabin and brought to potlucks and powwows? What was her secret; what wasn't she telling?

~ ~ ~

Three of the Dionne sisters, Yvonne, Annette, and Cecile, drove their ancient mother from the other side of the reservation, almost to the border between Mozhay and town, one morning to pay a call on Margie. As they passed the Reservation Business Committee building, Dale Ann, the Mozhay Point tribal education director and oldest of the Dionne girls, glanced out of her office window and recognized Annette's car careening off the road to take the shortcut through the Ar-Bee-See driveway and onto the road that led to Sweetgrass. "Ni misay-ag, ondii gidizhaa? Sisters, where are you going to?" she said aloud, ducking behind the blinds. Knowing that the road to Sweetgrass crossed the southernmost corner of the LaForce allotment she called to alert Margie, who then called her ladyfriend Theresa to come to the little house for a woman party. Margie and Theresa were ready for company and waiting at the door when the car drove up the driveway through the sumac stand that obscured the house from the road.

The sisters opened the car doors, which let in the mysterious and elusive scent of sweetgrass that floated on the lightest of breezes to tease their noses; the Dionne women inhaled deeply, turning their heads to follow the scent, to capture it; the intake calmed their demeanors, which became nearly consistently pleasant for the time that they were on the LaForce family allotment grounds.

Theresa waved hugely. "Mino giizhigad, Margie; it's the Dionne ladies!"

"Aneen, Margie; aneen, Theresa; it is good to see you," they said, sweet as boiled-down sap. "We were just taking Mother for a little ride, and when we saw you were home we decided to stop by."

"Biindigen gaye namadabin . . ." While Margie welcomed the women and found them comfortable places to sit (near the door for Yvonne, who suffered from hot flashes; next to the stove for Annette, who was always cold), Theresa switched on the Mr. Coffee and set the kettle on the stove for tea. Courteously she asked about Mrs. Dionne's bad knee, and if she liked her new washing machine, and how all of the grandchildren and great-grandchildren were while she poured coffee, and hot water, and offered sugar and milk (Cecile reminded Margie and Theresa that she couldn't tolerate dairy at all).

"Would you ladies eat a little frybread if I mix some up?" asked Margie. The ladies thought they could, if the pieces weren't too big. "And how is Dale Ann?" she asked, lifting the mixing bowl from the bottom cupboard.

"Yes, what is Big Sister up to?" Theresa inquired. "Busy all the time these days, I'll bet, eh?" She settled into her chair to observe the Dionnes while they watched Margie prepare a batch of frybread.

Old Lady Dionne took half-milk and half-coffee with four sugars, which she stirred for a full minute. "Nice and hot," she complimented, wrapping her cup in a napkin to lift it. "S'good; you girls make good coffee. My big girl? Oh, she's busy, mm hmm . . . working, taking care of things all over the reservation; but you know, no matter how busy she gets she always makes the time for me, whatever I need." She sighed happily; then, "Annette, get me something for my feet," she said impatiently.

"There's no more chairs," Annette said critically, then remembered where she was and what she wanted, and smiled stiffly at the room. "I don't think." Her dimples all but creaked.

"Here you go, Auntie Grace." Theresa put her own chair under the old woman's legs, first padding it with her sweater. "Is that better?"

"You're a good girl, Theresa. Now, what was I saying? Oh, I remember . . . yes, Big Sister, busy all over the reservation. She always did make us proud, always doing something nice for somebody. Had that good job, and then she went back to school, and she was so smart she made us all proud there, and then she . . ."

"She was way too busy to get married," muttered Yvonne.

"Even if somebody would have asked her," whispered Cecile.

"Gaazhigens, gi wi minikwe ina doodooshaboo?" asked Annette. *Cat, you want some milk to drink?*

". . . and all those little kids, my, she treated them just like they were her own . . . but now that she's in charge of all that education she's got so much going on with everything she has to do, she just doesn't have much time to be at Head Start anymore . . . those little kids, they all love her; they must really miss her . . . she stops by sometimes, though."

While their mother talked, the Dionne girls sugared their tea and coffee, then let it go cold, ignoring it to watch closely as

Margie worked, intending once and for all to discover what was the secret ingredient in the dough that she mixed and handled. They saw nothing unusual, just the mixing of the ingredients that could be found in their own kitchen cupboards. What sleight of hand was Margie using? What motions did she make that were quicker than the eye?

~ ~ ~

The frybread was as always delectable, perhaps even more than usual, this time perhaps too good to even dunk.

Yvonne had a lot of pride, which could be either a strength or the source of occasional but regular downfalls (she knew that and was too proud to change), but she humbled herself to ask if Margie would write down the recipe. Here is what Margie wrote:

FRYBREAD

Almost two cups of flour
Almost a tablespoon of b.p.
Pretty small-size pinch of salt
A little sugar, maybe a teaspoon (this
is up to you if you want it)

Mix this in a good-size bowl, and then make a little river, in a circle. Add warm water to make the dough nice and soft. Cover and give it a little rest after you mix.

Fry it like doughnuts. Good with butter, or honey, or jelly, or syrup. Or plain.

This makes a good lugallette, too. For lug, bake it in a pan. Cut it up.

But grease the pan first.

Away from the spell of Sweetgrass, the demeanor of the Dionne girls returned to its norm. In the front seat Yvonne and Annette argued over the radio, first one and then the other punching the selection button every few minutes to switch from country western to oldies, oldies to country western. In the back seat Cecile fidgeted indignantly until her mother told her to sit still, she was making her carsick.

"Anyhow, that's the way we always make it, just the same way Margie did," Annette complained. "Well, next time we'll use yeast instead of baking powder, or else soda. Maybe that's what she's doing. Maybe she's been using all three."

Yvonne wondered if it was Margie's stove. "Notice she never makes it anyplace else but at her own house?"

"And that Theresa, sitting there like that all smiling and just quiet. You know she knows all about it." Yvonne expressed this indignantly.

"And after her stealing Margie's man, too; why would Margie ever even talk to her?" The vision that crossed Annette's mind and eyes of Michael Washington as a young man diverted her attention, the car swerved slightly, and in the back seat Cecile squealed.

"Sister, watch your driving there; you want to go right off the road?" she snapped. The car righted; she tossed her head. "Well, Margie sure showed her! Who gets to be the big boss lady at Chi Waabik? Not Theresa!"

"Michael probably helped her get that job; he owes her plenty."

"Not to mention his father, and all I can say is, it's a good thing her frybread is as soft as it is, otherwise that old Zho Washington would probably have starved to death on the rest of her cooking."

Cecile grumbled, "She snuck something in there when we weren't looking. She's just a stingy-gut, that Margie, keeping her stupid secret to herself. Well, she can just have it."

Old Lady Dionne told her girls that Margie had made the frybread as she always had, with the same results, and that perhaps it was jealousy that was causing their bread to toughen and shrink.

Jealousy? Jealousy! Without speaking aloud the sisters agreed to silence in the car for the remainder of the ride back to the Dionne allotment, and Annette turned up Garth Brooks.

Here is part of Margie's secret: Unrequited love. The La-Force family land allotment in Sweetgrass. And not too much sugar when you add that little bit. But without Zho Washington's grandmother, the three would have remained unconnected, as would have the ingredients that went into Margie's mixing bowl and came out frybread, as would have the ingredients that went into her existence and came out Margie's life.

In Her Dream, Margie

1998

THE YOUNG MARGIE ROBINEAU moving through the landscape of her early-morning dream knew as well as would a much older woman all the songs and where they ended. She had danced this one a hundred times. As it neared the tail, the last minute of the fugue of drumbeat and voices, she danced nearer to the men at the drum, who in anticipation of the quickening of the pace leaned forward on their folding chairs. The lead singer bent to pick a Styrofoam cup up from the floor with his left hand, his right hand holding the drumstick in midair as he swallowed a mouthful of water between skipped beats. He cupped his left hand to his ear to hear as he raised his voice, the pitch a wolf singing into the wind, striking the drum harder with every other beat, volume muffled by the sheepskin wrapping on the end of the drumstick to a deep *boom!* felt by the girl who was Margie-enjiss at the back of the curved arabesque of her ribs as she danced. She watched Zho Wash's head bob, *now*, his white hair reflecting the fluorescent lighting of the gymnasium ceiling to the silver of Lost Lake under a full moon in winter, *now*, as the fugue dipped, bent, turned the corner into the tail of the song. *Now.*

The girl's gaze turned from the singers to the blur of the powwow circle, then inward. Her feet stayed with the drum, out of her sight but seen in her mind as she danced, moccasins beaded in blue skies and rivers, green leaves and vines, flowers the color of late summer, prancing and stepping, kicking and turning, sending her prayers to the Creator by way of skies and rivers, leaves, vines, and flowers of late summer. When the song ended, her practiced feet neatly hit the ground on the last beat, side by side, together, toes first, heels grounded on the last split second. *Hey, wuh.* Zho Wash didn't say it aloud.

~ ~ ~

She woke to the hesitant gurgle of the toilet flushing weak and thin on the other side of her bedroom wall as the middle-aged Margie who duct-taped her arch supports into her dance boots as she dressed for Grand Entry and who needed more than six hours of sleep. Half-opening her eyes to the osmotic fogginess of the beginnings of illumination, that gray light that seeps into rooms where morning sleepers endeavor to extend the night, she blinked at probing fingers of reality forcing daylight through slats of drawn vinyl window blinds, prying apart the crack between drawn curtains. Did I dance like that? she wondered. Am I young? No, she remembered; I have a daughter older than I was in the dream.

Crystal jiggled the flush handle to stop the irritatingly apologetic sound of the running toilet; she coughed, deep and dry. Rustled cellophane, her pack of Camels. Lit a match, phfft, sucked smoke, exhaled. Passing the bedroom door, she looked in to see if her mother was awake. Her left hand was cupped over her mouth, cigarette between her second and third fingers, filter close to her lips.

Margie saw the old man's silhouette, short-legged and skinny, with those stringy, muscular arms, standing in the doorway to the bedroom, gray and indistinct. An apparition. Zho Wash? Margie rubbed the back of her wrist against her eyes. The apparition stretched, crossed its wrists above its head, and became her daughter. I'm in Aunt Beryl's trailer, she remembered, not in the

allotment house. I live here; Zho lives at the hospital, in Convalescent Care.

"You up?" Crystal asked. "How late did you work?"

"Almost two. Busy at Chi-Waabik last night. Where were
you?"

"Out."

"With who?"

"Just out." She glared at her mother, none of your business.
"Did you find out about blackjack training?" Coughed. Dropped
her cigarette.

"Watch the rug! No, they haven't decided yet if they're gonna
have the class. Where's Aunt Beryl?"

"Down at the boat landing. Hey, I'm gonna go down there,
see if I can find a ricing partner. Can I borrow the rowboat, use
Michael's stuff, his duckbill and knockers? I know he's not there."
I'm broke.

You look like hell; who would want to rice with you? "Are you
hungover?"

"What do you think?" Crystal gulped, swallowing back the
dry heaves.

"Go ahead; it's Michael's stuff, not mine. Take whatever you
want; he's not around."

The young woman went back into Beryl's frilly bathroom.
She ran water noisily into the sink while she retched, took deep
breaths to settle her stomach. Pepto-Bismol, she thought. There
was a bottle in the medicine cabinet. She took two chalky pep-
permint swallows from the bottle and retched again, knelt on the
floor to see if she had heaved pink liquid on the matching pink
shag bathmat. She held a wet washcloth over her face, counted to
ten, and, cautiously, stood. Lifting the washcloth, she saw herself,
slack-faced, staring from out of the mirror with eyes that looked
like two pee holes in the snow, as Margie would say. Above the
reflection's shoulder two impossibly pretty Indians embraced, a

vaguely effeminate brave and a Nordic-featured princess simpering in front of a pink and gold sunset. Aunt Beryl had won the laminated plaque at Saturday Night Fever Bingo and hung it in the bathroom where it could be seen twice, on the wall and in the mirror. "Yech," she muttered. She sipped water from the plastic cup shaped like a rosebud.

"Crystal," her mother said when she came out of the bathroom, "I've been thinking about us moving back into the allotment house. Michael is just about never there; even when he is, he sleeps in the shed most of the time, anyway."

"It doesn't even have a furnace."

"But even in winter it's plenty warm with the woodstove, and then we'd have our own place; we did fine there before we moved in with Aunt Beryl. We could take care of it, you and me. It just needs a little work."

And take a chance on running into Michael, that bum who couldn't be bothered with his own daughter? "It's a wreck. It has raccoons under the stairs. Gawd. No, thanks. Let Michael deal with that place. Beryl needs you."

"Now while the weather's still nice we could try it again, Crystal. Do a little work and get it ready for winter. Zho Wash would like that."

"Gawd. I'm going to the landing." Crystal picked up her cigarettes and lighter from the kitchen counter and walked out, letting the door slam. At the bottom of the steps she spun around and went back into the kitchen to take her plaid flannel shirt from the hook by the door and a piece of leftover frybread from the bowl on the table.

"That's yesterday's," cautioned Margie.

"I'll eat it before I get to the road." Crystal squeezed her mother's shoulder. "You know the cabin's a dump. See you later."

At the bottom of the stairs she called back, "They better let you into blackjack training, those bastards. If they're letting

Theresa do it, they better let you, too." She walked as she always did, quickly, impatiently, with a long, short-legged stride, down the driveway and to the road.

As Margie absentmindedly bit into a piece of day-old frybread she wondered to herself when the cabin's barrel stove had last been cleaned and if the back door had been properly latched. "One of the worst jobs to do once it gets cold, cleaning up a dirty stove in a freezing room," she said to herself. "Even worse job if a raccoon gets in." She microwaved a cup of instant coffee, positioned her arch supports into Zho Wash's old moccasins that waited for her feet; then, still in her pajamas, sat outside on the log-splitting stump, dunking day-old frybread and contemplating the cut-off path that led from Beryl's trailer back to the LaForce allotment house.

The Art of Dressing a Rabbit

1971

ON THE FIRST DAY OF FALL QUARTER Michael Washington,
the first member of the Washington and Dommage families to set
foot in a college, walked into the "Indians of America" class and
sat in the center of the back row, armed for the struggle with the
unknown with a GED, a spiral notebook, and a leaky blue ball-
point pen. His wallet held a Duluth Transit Authority bus pass,
his new student identification card, his draft card, a small photograph of his mother, taken at a Woolworth store booth in Minneapolis, and nearly two hundred dollars in cash, what remained
from his state Indian scholarship check after he had paid tuition
and a dormitory room deposit. It was the most money he had
ever held at one time, and although it had to stretch for books as
well as the rest of his fall quarter expenses, it had seemed, at first,
a fortune. However, since arriving at school and deciding to save
money by not buying a meal plan, he had spent two dollars at the
dorm cafeteria for a supper with unlimited helpings, then the next
night three dollars for a pizza. He was going to have to find a job.

In the next ten minutes the Washington and Dommage families' educational stalking horse daydreamed of the part-time job
he would find to supplement his scholarship and what he might
spend his money on: the Ponderosa Steak House, movies, perhaps

that sweater for his mother, the red one with the turtleneck that she had admired in Dayton's window display. As he pondered his financial prospects he watched college students, all to Michael's eyes white and all in pairs or groups, walking into the classroom and settling into all but the first and last rows of auditorium-style seats. At one minute before ten o'clock the professor *lady in a Pendleton blanket made into some sort of cape* entered the front of the room from a side door and sighed at the untimeliness of John Lennon, who at the same moment strolled in through the back door and sat at the end of row ten, nodding to Michael and raising one hand in a peace sign. The professor raised her attendance sheet and took a breath; five seconds into class time the last student rushed into the classroom and into the empty seat at the other end of the back row. Michael glanced at the young woman who settled her purse and tote bag on the floor *embarrassed; tall.* She turned to Michael, pushing back her jacket hood, and an Indian girl, the first one he'd seen all day, raised her eyebrows and smiled. "Whew," she said.

The professor was a graying white woman with a thin neck that drooped forward over a bony concave bosom, pulled by the weight of a hefty Navajo squash blossom necklace. She had bargained an elderly man down to a hundred dollars for the necklace during her summer research trip to Arizona; fingering the nali, silver worn and warmed over decades to a near-white patina, she thought of desert winters, of retirement, and of how tired she was of lecturing to class after class of sluggish students who had no interest in her scholarship. She sighed again, at the empty first row, then at eight tiers of students (mediocre, she thought; ordinary, all of them) up to the center of the tenth and highest row where her eyes stopped at what she had hoped without hope to see for the past two years she had taught "Indians of America": an authentic Indian-looking brave. She began to read from the list name after name, "Aho . . . Carlson . . . Floyd . . ." Who was the young man who bore a resemblance to Jay Silverheels, or was it Marlon Brando? "Rooney . . ."

The young woman in the back row cleared her throat. "Here," she responded in a slightly nasal soprano. The professor who under other circumstances might have noted an American Indian student's presence with a small penciled asterisk on the list had eyes only for Sal Mineo, or was it George Hamilton, and read on all the way to the W's, with each name slightly inclining her head at *the handsome Indian warrior, the young chief,* the student high above her head in the back row and at the end of the alphabet until at last he answered "here" in a thrilling monotone to the last name on her list: Michael Washington.

"Welcome. Welcome to 'Indians of America.' I am Dr. Rogers-Head." The professor's voice was loud and sharp. "What is your band?" she asked the student in the middle of row ten. The heads of the students in rows two through nine turned as though all nailed to one lath to see who she was addressing.

"Uh, Miskwaa River, that was my mother's band," a real live Indian of America answered.

"Ah, the Miskwaa River Band." She paused, shook her head. "Such tragic victimization at the hands of American imperialism." Pressing her lips together, the professor nodded, pulled her head back and up, *a bridled horse,* drew in a deep breath slightly larger in volume than her nostrils.

Michael nodded politely in return; the young woman at the end of row ten slouched low in her seat, lower.

The remainder of the lecture continued to be directed toward row ten, seat twelve. Michael stopped listening after the first intense ninety seconds but continued to answer with courteous nods from time to time. When the professor turned away to write on the blackboard, he drew in his spiral notebook figures of Indians, dogs, and arrows, occasionally blotting the end of the leaky pen in the margins.

In row 10, seat 24, the other Indian student, her attention on Michael as intense as Dr. Rogers-Head's, kept her eyes down and wrote steadily with a brand-new pencil in a loose-leaf binder as she watched him nod in response each time the professor paused and sought his collusion:

Christopher Columbus
Custer's Last Stand
Rape and slaughter
Establishment
War machine
  soda crackers
  7-Up
  deodorant
Margie, Jupiter—can I use her discount

After class the professor rushed out the front door and around to the door at the back of the classroom. She stepped in front of Michael and told him that she admired the statement he made with his hair.

Michael mumbled. She sniffed, cleared her throat, gestured toward his head. Silver and turquoise bracelets that hung from the dead tree branch that was her wrist clanked and jangled.

"By wearing your hair long you are making the assertion that you are, yourself, a warrior embodiment of rage against the oppressions of the establishment. I look forward to the contribution you will make to the course. The students will at last have the opportunity to see and hear from one who has experienced firsthand the degradations and injustices of the military-industrial complex!" Her nostrils enthusiastically whistled, vibrated. "I did graduate fieldwork at the Standing Rock Reservation. The Sioux men are very much like you."

"Mm hmm." Michael pondered his answer, inhaled to reply, and the professor whirled; the Pendleton slid off one shoulder; she snapped one end across her chest and over the other shoulder, strode several long steps in buckled Pilgrim-style brogues, and paused. Her head swiveled, owl-like *eyes that would freeze a rabbit.* "We'll no doubt talk again!" A half dozen more steps and a turn to the left; the Pendleton swung out at a right angle to the floor and vanished around a corner.

"Good-bye, then," Michael answered politely to empty air.

Theresa, who had been waiting in the doorway of the classroom across the hall, smiled at Michael. "Boozhoo," she said.

"Boozhoo."

"Hard to keep up with her, taking notes, hmm?" During Dr. Rogers-Head's lecture she had watched Michael draw four pictures and print one word: his name, gripped in the talons of a flying eagle. "Talks pretty fast; did you get a lot down?" Her voice was a light tap on his breastbone, her eyes long black triangles near laughter. "Want to copy my notes? My name's Theresa, Theresa Rooney."

"Michael Washington."

She invited him to supper, which she would cook on the hot plate in her rented room.

~ ~ ~

At the boardinghouse, Theresa turned the key, rattled the doorknob. Pushed. "Well, this is it," she said, opening the door. Her fingers brushed the wall *the sound of moth wings against thinly veneered paneling*, then a light switch clicked and sparked. Overhead a yellowed glass square the size and pattern of a handkerchief dingily lit a large upright mirrored bureau, a bookshelf, a greasy-looking brown tweed La-Z-Boy recliner, and a double bed covered with a white chenille bedspread.

"Nice place," complimented Michael. Bigger than his half of the dormitory room, nicer than his mother's bedroom, the only one in their apartment in Minneapolis, and quieter. There was just about enough room for another person to sleep on the floor, if she should be looking for a roommate . . .

"Gets chilly when I'm gone." She turned the knob at the bottom of the radiator, which began to clatter, with a faint whistle. Below, rusty water dripped into a coffee can on a warped and stained linoleum floor.

"Here, you want to help?" She handed him mushroom soup, tuna, peas, a can opener. "You can drain the tuna and peas in the bathroom; it's at the end of the hallway," she directed. On the burner she boiled water and added Minute Rice, then the soup, the drained tuna, and finally the peas.

Theresa's back was to Michael as she stirred the mixture gently, taking care not to break the peas. He was able to watch her shift from left foot to right, reach to the bookshelf for the pepper, tap the spoon against the rim of the saucepan to loosen the food, hold one hand over the pan to feel the heat, lean forward to smell. The girl's jeans were worn to a sandpapered-looking pale blue in the seat, which bagged slightly below her flat behind and skinny hips; a missing pocket had left an unfaded darker blue chevron shape on the rear; the side seams were frayed, and the hems had been patched and lengthened. New-looking clogs added inches to her height; her eyes were on the same level as Michael's, he had noticed as he handed her the drained cans of peas and tuna. Her hair was a curtain, straight but crimped below the shoulders with waves and ridges from the braids she wore to bed; it covered her back nearly to her waist, swaying back and forth fluidly over her torso as she worked.

"Here you go." Theresa handed Michael a plastic bowl and a restaurant's fork. "It's hot, anyway." She ate directly from the saucepan with the mixing spoon.

"This is pretty good, Theresa," Michael said. "You're a good cook."

"Oh, I get that from my mother: she can cook with anything, and it always turns out. You should visit her with me sometime; she lives here in Duluth. At Capehart—the base housing—you know where that is? My dad's in the Philippines; he's in the Air Force."

So this girl had some money, Michael thought. One of the rich Indian girls.

"Hey, same here; you should come visit my mother, if you ever get to the Cities. My mom is Lucy Dommage. She's a Mozhay Pointer; that's where she was born."

Noticing that Michael had eaten all of his supper, Theresa spooned the last of the meal from the saucepan to his bowl. "My girlfriend Margie Robineau, her family is from Mozhay. The La-Forces. Do you know them?"

"The LaForces? Ha! That's where my dad is! He lives there on their property, in the old allotment house. No kidding!" Did she have a roommate? Michael looked around, surreptitiously, he hoped.

"Oh, do you know Margie, then?"

"No, never met her. They don't live on the allotment, the La-Forces, except for their aunt Beryl; she lives on the property, in a trailer down the road from us. You should come up to Mozhay Point—know where the allotment is, at Sweetgrass? We could both go up there; you could meet my dad, he likes company." Michael finished the last forkful of rice and tuna. A good meal, but he was still hungry. "Hey, you like rabbit?"

"I've never had rabbit. I heard it tastes like chicken," she flirted, catching his eyes, raising her eyebrows and turning ever so slightly sideways.

"Never had rabbit? What kind of Indian are you? Where are you from?"

"My grandpa was from Warroad, and what do you mean what kind of Indian? I'm the kind that can make frybread to go with that cooked-up rabbit." For the first time Theresa looked directly at Michael.

Had he gotten her mad? Time to try a joke. "Waaboos, it's the Chippewa national dish; can't be a Chippewa if you don't eat rabbit."

Time to get the guy in line. "What about macaroni? Don't you know you can't be an Indian if you don't eat your macs?"

He tried again. "Did you ever hear how the Sioux always say that our national anthem is 'Here Comes Peter Cottontail'?"

This made Theresa laugh aloud, which inspired Michael to tell another. "We're just joking when we do that, those Chippewa and Sioux jokes. You know we used to be at war with each other in the old days, long time ago? But now we don't mean anything by it . . ."

Theresa raised one eyebrow. *What makes you think I don't know this?*

". . . so, know what the Sioux national anthem is? It's 'How Much Is That Doggie in the Window'!" He laughed so hard that he coughed.

"You want some water?"

"No, a smoke." He flipped one from the end of the pack he took from his shirt pocket, tapped the filter end against the back of one hand to concentrate the tobacco. "Sagaswaa?"

He was finally flirting back, what a relief. "What's that?"

"That means cigarette; smoking. Want a smoke?"

"I don't smoke, but I like the way it smells. I love standing next to somebody who's smoking."

He really liked this girl, Michael thought to himself.

Before he left, he said, "I really meant it, you're welcome to come up to Sweetgrass; that's where the cabin is. We'll snare some rabbits, and my dad'll make some rabbit stew. You'll like that."

"And I'll make frybread. Can I bring Margie?"

"Well, I don't know . . . does she like the smell of cigarettes?"

Is she a rich Indian girl, too?

~ ~ ~

On the second day of class and Michael's last day of college he looked up from his spiral notebook to the blackboard, which Dr. Rogers-Head was tapping with the end of a stick of chalk. In block letters she had printed:

THE INDIAN RELIGION

The professor pressed her backside into the chalk tray. "My great-great-grandmother was the daughter of a Cherokee chief," she announced, gesturing like Debra Paget and crossing her arms. As she paused her bracelets shivered and grew momentarily still.

Theresa slumped in her chair and began to draw. "I've heard this one before," she muttered.

Dr. Rogers-Head turned to write on the board. The chalk tray had left a wide stripe of white chalk dust across the rear of her dark wool skirt.

"Shigog," thought Michael; *skunk.*

There was a ripple, the beginning of laughter, from somewhere in the middle in the lecture hall.

"I think she's really a Chalk-taw," Theresa whispered under her breath. The professor pivoted her owl-head to glare at the class while her body continued to face the blackboard. The room quieted.

"Chi-ko-ko-koho," thought Michael; *owl. Scared them to sleep.* For the rest of the hour he sat as still as a stone. When class ended he was the first student out the door, walking quickly down the hall away from the professor's office and around the opposite corner. Safe, he waited for Theresa.

"Rooney," he whispered.

The girl stopped.

"Got something for you." He tore a page from his spiral notebook and handed it to the girl. On the top line he had written "Joseph Washington" and below that a map from Duluth to Mozhay Point reservation, to Sweetgrass, to the LaForce land allotment and the allotment house.

"I'm going out to buy some cigarettes," he told Theresa. "See you later." The next time she saw him would be the winter day she talked Margie into driving up north to the reservation.

~ ~ ~

After stopping at the dorm to pick up his clothes, Michael used a pay phone to call himself at his mother's apartment.

"I have a collect person-to-person call for Michael Washington," the operator announced in her flat working voice. "Will you accept the charges?"

"He's not here," answered Lucy.

"He is not there," relayed the operator to the caller, who was Michael. "Sir, would you like to leave a callback number?"

"Just tell him I'm going up north, and . . ."

The operator cut off the call. "Sir . . ." she said reproachfully as she returned his dime.

Michael hung up and then walked to the Miller Trunk to hitchhike his way north to Sweetgrass.

~ ~ ~

The Jupiter store in downtown Duluth, wedged between Baker's Shoes and a small print shop on Superior Street, was not as large, bright, or well-stocked as the Woolworth's at the end of the block (called Big Woolworth's by Duluthians in order to distinguish it from the smaller Little Woolworth's at the other end of downtown). Jupiter customers moved more slowly than Woolworth customers; they didn't ask for much and had developed a culture of down-at-the-heels camaraderie and rather courtly courtesy, which was the reason for underdog Jupiter's survival in the face of Woolworth big business.

The elderly man in the storm coat climbing wearily onto the stool at the Jupiter lunch counter was so bent over that his long, rather silky white eyebrows nearly brushed the rim of his coffee cup, set before him by the time he lifted his sore and swollen feet to the rail beneath the counter.

"Thank you, miss . . . it surely does smell good in here." He reached for the sugar and cream that Margie carefully slid to within his stiff and limited reach.

"Do you want the hamburger sandwich, Mr. Hansen?" she asked. It was Tuesday, the day for the old man's weekly labored trip down the stairs from his room above the Used-a-Bit store and down the avenue to the Jupiter for his one extravagance: a 25-cent sandwich and a 15-cent cup of coffee, refilled as often as he liked by his favorite waitress, the Indian girl who cooked and served so fetchingly behind the lunch counter. Today, he noticed, she was wearing her half-slip, not the full one, which meant that when she turned her back he would be able to see her brassiere through her white nylon uniform.

She had been hired for the lunch counter job not long after failing a quarter at the local college, and in the months since had grown to look forward to the Tuesday morning routine: Mr. Hansen arrived before eleven o'clock in order to not have to share her attention during the lunch rush; he asked if she had a newspaper; she borrowed a morning *News-Tribune* from the stand in front of the store and propped it against the sugar shaker on the counter to the left of the old man's coffee, folded in half and smoothed for ease in handling and reading. This morning, as it was every Tuesday morning, while Margie continued her routine (scooping a handful of ground meat from the bin in the cooler, buttering the grill, warming a thick white plate in the oven), she missed the part of the routine most important to Mr.

Hansen, which was that while she prepared his lunch he secretly imagined that the day was a Sunday and himself back thirty years at the kitchen table in his own house drinking coffee and waiting for breakfast, watching and listening to his wife work while he looked over the paper.

Margie fried a generous third-pound of hamburger, which was a little more than the scant quarter-pound the other customers got, and because poor Mr. Hansen couldn't eat onions and because of his high blood pressure, she seasoned the meat with just the slightest shake of salt for flavor as well as a pinch of cinnamon, which gave it an aroma and flavor somewhat like Margie's memories of her mother's Canadian pork pies. As Margie worked the meat with a wooden spoon and metal spatula, turning and separating it to well-done crumbles, she inhaled the familiar scent that rose from the steaming grill and, like Mr. Hansen, imagined a woman at work in a kitchen: Margie's mother, gently patting rolled-out dough into a pie pan in preparation for the fragrant cinnamon-and-nutmeg spiced meat, the moment an intertwining of grief with the comfort that a motherless girl gleans from her dreams.

The hamburger fried, Margie buttered two slices of the softest Taystee bread from the middle of the loaf; gently, she scooped the pile of meat between the slices and shaped it with her hands to a cohesiveness that Mr. Hansen could manage. She arranged half the sandwich on a thick white plate next to a scoop of cottage cheese, another unauthorized substitution for Mr. Hansen because he couldn't eat potato chips, and neatly wrapped the other half in a sheet of waxed paper.

Mr. Hansen ate and read, then put the wrapped half-sandwich in his pocket for later on and stiffly, painfully, stood three-quarters erect. He laid four dimes and two nickels on the counter. "That was delicious, young lady. Thank you. And keep the change. Buy yourself something."

As he shuffled his way toward the front of the Jupiter, a young woman entered. He gallantly held the door open; more accurately but unseen by Mr. Hansen, she provided needed leverage with her elbow while he held the handle. Because of the bend in his back and shoulders, the old man's vision when he stood was usually limited to the ground and what might be at most people's waist level; his interaction and conversation with others was almost nonexistent. He sensed a pretty girl and expected to be ignored, but this one curtsyed slightly, bringing her face to his level, and smiled. Her teeth were even and white, her eyes almond-shaped and playful, and her long dark hair shone with red highlights. "Thank you," she said as though he were the strongest man in the world. He smelled perfume that seemed to rise *from a fine bosom, not too big and not too small, he thought.* "You are most welcome," he replied. *This is a good day, well worth the walk.*

~ ~ ~

"Hi, Theresa. You want a Coke?"

"A glass of water. You don't care if I eat my crackers here, do you? . . . and wait 'til you hear this: I met this guy, and his dad lives up at Mozhay Point, you'll never guess where, and he invited us up . . ."

It was going to be lots of fun, Theresa told Margie. Theresa would drive and Margie wouldn't even have to chip in for gas, unless she really wanted to. Had Margie ever been up to her family's land allotment? The guy she'd met, Michael, really wanted them to come up for a visit. His dad would cook rabbit soup. Why did they call the place "Sweetgrass"; could they pick some? Maybe they could try to make some of those little sweetgrass baskets; did Margie know how?

"They call it 'Sweetgrass' because you can really smell it all round, but nobody can ever find it; that's what I've heard. I don't know anybody who knows how to sew those baskets."

Theresa was going to make frybread; wouldn't Margie like to cook, too? Had Margie ever tried rabbit?

"Rabbit, yes, I have," Margie answered, and clicked her tongue, thinking that skinned, they looked like cats, or babies. When she cooked rabbit she always cut the limbs apart and the meat from the limbs without looking directly at what she was doing and had developed unusually good peripheral vision. "Lots of times. It's all dark meat; I don't know if you'd like it. I don't, especially."

"Well, come with, anyway. Michael said we can meet his dad, and they live in the old cabin that's been there for years. Have you ever seen it?"

"The old house? No, I don't remember it. I've been up to the allotment but not since before my mother died; I must have been four or five the last time we were there. My dad's aunt Beryl lives down the road, but I don't even remember how to get there. And I have to work, Theresa; I can't just take off."

"We'll go on a day you don't have work, and we can meet Michael somewhere, and he'll show us where it is, and it'll be lots of fun, Margie, you'll see. Come on; let's go. We'll be back by that same night. Please, Margie, don't make me go alone."

~ ~ ~

"This must be the Dionne Fork. Look, there he is!"

Michael was waiting for them outside of Tuomela's Gas and Grocery, a Skelly station across from the Dionne family allotment, where the dirt road to the reservation branched off from the blacktopped county highway. At first to Margie he was only a dark and bulky silhouette against a dirty white snowbank, smoking a cigarette that glowed orange on the end. As they drove closer the silhouette became Michael, dressed in a heavy winter jacket, with long hair that the wind whipped into writhing black snakes that lashed his shoulders and blew in all directions from his head, twining and untwining, tangling and straightening. He saw Theresa's car and threw the cigarette into the snowbank, waving to the cashier inside the gas station, a girl with black-framed, large-lensed Indian Health Service–issue eyeglasses. She was rubbing at the window with a fistful of wadded newspaper, peering closely at a large smear of Brylcreem left by her cousin Eugene, who had leaned back against the glass when he had stopped by to visit earlier.

"See you, Dale Ann," Michael called to the girl in the window, but because the wind swallowed his words she didn't hear, and because the wind drove those snakes across his face, covering it, she didn't see his mouth form the words. She waved anyway, with the hand holding the newspaper; with the other she pushed her heavy glasses up higher on her nose.

Michael walked toward the car, dancing to keep his balance against the push of the wind and elegant in his clumsy thick jacket. As he walked he gathered his hair into one fist and pushed it down into his collar. When he opened the back door and ducked into the car, he nodded toward the front seat, at Theresa and her girlfriend. Cold, smoke-scented air brushed Margie's face.

"Rooney. Boozhoo." His voice was a low tenor, the pitch soft and indirect; it might have come from a distance, miles away, or years.

Theresa's hair, cared-for hair that was longer than Michael's and Margie's too, as well as shinier and softer, draped in a thick curve over the right side of her face when she turned to face the back seat. She drew it aside like a curtain, and Margie felt the mild sickness of envy. "Boozhoo! Margie, this is Michael."

"Nice to meet you." His smile was brilliant, even with his mouth nearly closed because of his bad teeth.

The closeness of Michael in the small car affected Margie in much the same way as decades later the remembered vision of young Michael affected Annette Dionne: if Margie were driving, the car would have swerved. "You, too," she answered faintly, tightly, her voice swallowed down into her throat by her shyness. She inhaled, hoped for more words but couldn't find a one, felt the car spin even as she saw through the curved glass of the windshield that the gas station stayed exactly where it was.

They drove on the dirt road into Sweetgrass, across the LaForce allotment lands: first Beryl's turquoise and silver trailer, farther down the road the turnoff to the old LaForce cabin where Michael's father lived, and finally the end of the road, near the popple stand where Earl and Alice LaForce, distant cousins to Margie's dad, lived in a former railroad pump car house. Margie spent the drive in tongue-tied silence. Envying her friend's social graces, she listened to Theresa talk about the weather, the uncertain future of her car's tires, that she was hungry for rabbit soup, a one-sided conversation that filled the car. In the back seat, Michael listened, nodded, responded "Mm hmm" every few minutes, and occasionally laughed.

A five-minute walk into the woods led to the snares, which were set in a line twenty feet out and parallel to the abandoned tracks. Margie had worn her father's wool lumberjack shirt and brought a pair of choppers and a watch cap borrowed from the lost and found box at Jupiter. Theresa had only the hooded jacket she was wearing; Margie gave the choppers to Theresa and pulled her own sweater sleeves and the cuffs of her father's jacket down over her hands. Michael, who had neither cap nor gloves, turned his jacket collar up to cover his ears. His exposed hands were graceful cedar carvings ornamented with calluses and chapped knuckles.

"If you girls get too cold, you can go back to the car." Following the snare line Michael walked ahead, in front of the girls, who huddled with linked arms for warmth, back of his shoulders. His steps were deliberate; his boots, ancient black rubber galoshes tied with twine, broke tracks through the ice-encrusted snow. Margie stepped next, into his tracks, walking nearly sideways under the weight and pull of Theresa's shivering arm. Michael's hair, loosed from his coat collar, separated again into black strings that snapped in the wind; once, when he paused and Margie came close to walking into his back, the ends brushed her face. Theresa, in platform clogs and with her hood pulled tightly around her face, balanced on crane legs, tottered unevenly, nearly leaping from track to track to keep up with the pace set by short-legged Margie and Michael. "Holy, I'm getting hungry," she muttered. "Hope we find one pretty soon."

The first three snares were empty; the fourth was not. Michael stepped between the girls and the kicking, dying rabbit, turning his back to Margie and Theresa and bending to block the sight, to spare their eyes. "I hate it when this happens," he said. His soft voice was husky and sad.

From back of Michael's shoulders Margie saw his elbows move quickly, twice, heard him sigh; then he lifted the snare with the still and relaxed body. He put the rabbit in a cloth sack that he took from his pocket, then took a pinch of tobacco from his shirt pocket and placed it on the ground next to the snare. For several seconds he was silent, praying his apology and appreciation, which was the traditional way and proper for an Ojibwe. Only then did he look up at Theresa and Margie. "You cold? Want to go home and eat?"

Back in the car they drove another half mile along the dirt road toward the LaForce allotment. At a driveway nearly hidden from the road by a stand of sumac and brush, Michael said, "Turn here, in here," and Margie laid eyes for the first time since she was a little girl on the LaForce house, built in the middle of the forty acres that had been allotted to her great-grandfather by the federal government more than three-quarters of a century before.

Michael's father got to his feet when the girls walked into the cabin, picking up his blanket from the wooden chair next to the woodstove where he had been sitting, the warmest spot in the room. He chivalrously spread the blanket on an old green velvet sofa over the stuffing and springs that were coming through the frays and rents in its lumpy cushions and pulled it closer to the stove. "Biindigen; namadabin," he murmured, nodding toward the sofa. "Come in, young ladies, and sit down. Here's a place for you."

His smile was almost as big as his head, thought Margie. What a nice old man. She stepped over the chainsaw that was lying on the floor half-wrapped in a tattered rag rug.

"This is Theresa, and Margie," Michael introduced them, indicating with his version of the old man's nod who was who. "This is my father. Joe Washington."

"I'm very happy to meet you, Mr. Washington." Theresa offered her hand to shake.

The old man glanced with appreciation at her high color, her nose and cheeks flushed with the cold, and her long, long black hair. A beauty; feels good on old eyes, he thought. "Boozhoo aniin. Likewise," he said, shaking her chilled and slender hand. "Everybody calls me Zho Wash." He regarded the other girl, the bashful one, gently and indirectly.

Margie smiled sideways at the old man. "Boozhoo." Then once again tongue-tied she smiled down at the floor, then back up at the old man, then again at the floor. The old man was in his socks, she saw; one toe stuck out of a hole in the side. She looked away; he quickly bent to pull the sock away from the foot, hiding his toe. All the while her eyes avoided Michael while she watched him with her unusually good peripheral vision.

Zho Wash thought, this one is crazy about my boy. "Boozhoo aniin, my girl. Here, you sit on the couch there; you'll warm up. Take your girlfriend with you. I'll make youse some tea."

While Michael was out on the front steps skinning the rabbit, Margie and Theresa sat on the couch with their coats over their laps watching the old man make tea. He lined three cups up on the table and filled them with hot water from the saucepan on the woodstove, then from the shelf above the table took down a box of Salada tea. He dipped a teabag up and down several times, into first one cup and then the second, which he handed to the girls. Zho Wash used the teabag for himself last; the hot water in the third cup was all but colorless and at that point not really tea; to get all that he could out of the bag he lifted it out with a fork and wound the string around and around, wringing the last drops into his cup. "Drink your tea; don't wait for me," he said to the girls as the string separated from the bag, spilling most of the bled leaves into the hot water.

They drank without talk in the quiet room, the girls sipping like ladies in the presence of gentlemanly Zho Wash. They could hear Michael outside on the steps, dressing the rabbit. Margie pictured his motions from the sounds she heard: he carried a board from the woodpile to the stairs, sat while he skinned the carcass with his hunting knife, removed and cleaned the head and tucked it into his jacket pocket, lay the carcass on the board while he separated the limbs and cut them into smaller cooking pieces. Threw the guts to Zho Wash's silent and deferential dogs. He stood, walked up the wooden stairs carrying the board like a tray, opened the door, walked into the room; cold, stinging little bits of ice and snow blew inside and melted on Margie's face that the heat of the stove and the tea, and her thoughts of Michael, had thawed from frosted yellow to peach pink.

"Nice and warm in here." The brilliance of Michael's smile was the white of enamel against the darkness of decay and missing teeth; it was the pleasure of preparing rabbit meat with skill; it was love for his father; it was stepping from the cold sun of outside into the woodsmoke-scented comfort of the dark cabin; it was light on Margie's face. "Meat's ready," he said.

To the feast Theresa had brought an onion; Margie, carrots. Zho Wash opened the back door from the cabin that led to an attached shed and pulled inside a nearly empty gunnysack. He squatted and dug, pulled out six potatoes, three in each hand. Theresa and Margie peeled and cut vegetables while the water heated on the woodstove; Michael and his father cut the rabbit meat from the bones and into cubes and slices that they seared in a frying pan and added once the vegetables were boiling.

Zho Wash discreetly left the house and disappeared into the woods while Michael and the girls were clearing the table and cleaning the kitchen. Hanging a saucepan on a nail next to the window, Theresa noticed the old man walking down the path away from the back door. "Where is your dad going?" she asked, then, remembering that the house didn't have a flush toilet, answered herself, "Oh."

While the soup simmered, Michael cooked the rabbit head, a treat for his father. Margie and Theresa watched as he fried the head, turning it over and over with a fork. The meat, the most tender part of the rabbit, sizzled and crispened in the reheated fat as the little head rolled around in the frying pan, and suddenly Theresa felt queasy. She sat on the end of the couch that turned her away from the stove and took several deep breaths of cabin air that had become heavy and close. Lightheaded, she opened the door.

Returning from the woods, Michael's father waved to the taller girl, who was leaning against the door frame. "Going outside?" he asked, thinking that she might be looking for the outhouse.

"No, just thinking how beautiful the woods are: the snow is so clean out here, and everything smells . . . refreshing," Theresa answered, swallowing a gasp.

"Feels like spring is coming, doesn't it? Namadabi daa; let's sit and take a rest. Let Michael finish the work."

Margie and Theresa looked with Zho Wash at the pictures he brought out from the bedroom, of two young women, his wives. He held out the first, a small portrait photograph framed in cardboard, carefully, the edges between a thumb and second finger.

"Genevieve; we used to call her Eva," Zho Wash introduced her.

Eva, before that little seedling of tuberculosis rooted in her chest grew and flowered, and her coughing separated the linings from her lungs, causing her at first a wet and bloody cough and then hemorrhage and death in the sanitarium, sat solemnly for the photographer with her hair bobbed and straight and her bangs straight and neat, wearing a white middy blouse and dark pleated skirt, her Haskell Indian Boarding School uniform.

"Pretty girl," commented Theresa.

The old man cleared his throat, looked at the picture and past it. "She died young, a long time ago," he said.

The second picture was newer, a snapshot in a handmade wooden frame. The girl behind the glass had been frozen by the camera in midstep, on one foot, with her hands in the pockets of her fur-collared storm coat, in front of the lighthouse on the pier in Duluth. Her head, with its World War II–era topknot and long pin-curled waves, was thrown back, her eyes nearly closed, black crescents dancing, balanced on high, sharp cheekbones. She was laughing.

"Lucy," Zho Wash said. "Michael's mother." With the girls he studied the snapshot.

"I think Michael looks just like her," said Theresa.

"Yes, he really does," said Margie, thinking more handsome than pretty. So that's Lucy, the one that took off. She had heard her aunts discussing Zho Wash's folly. What did he expect, they asked each other. He was too old for her and not much company for somebody her age, and she was wild anyway.

The old man carried the pictures back into the bedroom, where he carefully hung the portrait back on the wall and placed the snapshot frame on the wooden crate upended next to the bed.

Theresa and Margie were quiet; they had looked into the faces of girls who were no longer girls, one dead and one flown, and realized that at the moment the pictures were taken Eva and Lucy had had no more idea of what might come in their futures than they did their own at that moment sitting on the couch in Michael's father's house. As Zho Wash straightened the pictures in the bedroom, pulled the corners of the blankets on the bed tighter, moved his comb and nail clippers from the left to the right side of the dresser, the corners of Theresa's mouth tightened and Margie's lips pursed. Margie thought of her failed attempt at going to college, of her job at the lunch counter, loved yet linked to defeat, of myriad inadequacies and losses. Theresa thought of her mother who, alone and frightened in the absence of both husband and daughter, called the boardinghouse pay telephone at least twice every evening. Sometimes, when Theresa couldn't think of anything they might possibly talk about, Margie took the call and listened to loneliness in a one-way conversation, aching for her own mother.

Some of the girls they had known in high school were married, and some of them had babies. Margie and Theresa saw their own lives in comparison as frivolous and childish, lacking in the gravity of early adulthood; at the same time, some of those girls looked so tired, and their lives seemed toilsome. Wondering uneasily about a future that they were beginning to suspect was as unchangeable as the past, only less visible, they brooded, Margie and Theresa, mirroring one another, foreheads creasing and eyelids drooping, sad on the broken-down sofa across from the doorway to the bedroom, where the pensive old man rearranged his belongings.

"Soup smells like it's getting there," commented Michael, distracting them from their unhealthy thoughts by giving them something to do.

"Time to start the dough, then." Theresa cleared the table and braided her long hair to one side, then wrapped a flour sacking towel across her torso and *fine, not too big and not too small* bust, tying it in the back. She was ready to make frybread.

Back on the velvet couch Zho Wash began to talk about the time he'd spent in the South, after the war. He had seen an alligator, picked cotton. Went to a church once where a shouting woman wrapped a snake around her waist and prayed. Traveled around on the railroad in boxcars or a couple of times rode lying right on the rods underneath the cars.

"Under the train? That's got to be awful dangerous."

"Minawaa; what was that?" Yes, it was pretty dangerous to do that, ride the rods; have to hold on and keep your eyes shut because of the rocks and at the same time stay awake: if you go to sleep you fall off and get killed.

"There's a lot of black people in the South; you don't see many up here. They're a generous people; take you right into the house, share what they've got to eat with you. That's because a lot of them in that part of the country are part Indian, themselves. . . . They treated me good."

With her long brown hands Theresa mixed flour with the baking soda she'd brought, wrapped in a square of waxed paper in her jeans pocket, and added warm water and a pinch of salt. She had a light touch with frybread; her fingers danced and fluttered through the dough until it tasted of Theresa—a salty sweetness, Juicy Fruit gum, Emeraude cologne, and a hint of perspiration—and until it was just the consistency of that tender skin on the underside of a woman's arm, as she had learned from her mother. Taking care to not look at the fried rabbit head that Michael had set aside on a saucer for Zho to eat later on, she heated lard in the frying pan to near smoking, pulled pieces of dough the size of a small egg from the bowl, palmed each in her left hand, poked a little hole through the center with her right middle finger, laid it gently in the sizzling lard, turned it once with a fork. As the pieces browned she fished them out of the frying pan with the fork and set them to drain on a pile of folded newspapers.

Inches away from Theresa, Michael danced as he had with the wind, unaware that he swayed with her motions as she mixed, and kneaded, and shaped dough, and hovered between the frying pan and the newspaper. "Want some help, Theresa?"

"No, I think I'm about finished. Just have to wipe off the table so we can eat." Theresa's face was flushed and shiny with heat from the woodstove and from cooking; she had unbuttoned the top button of her blouse while she worked, and from the space between her breasts an almost visible steam of Emeraude and perspiration mingled with the sweet Juicy Fruit scent of her breath and the warm, enticing scent of frybread to rise and float over the table.

"Let me help you with that," Michael said.

"Oh, thanks," she answered, folding the corners of the newspapers and lifting them like a platter. The skin of Theresa's throat and upper chest was the same shade of gold as the piled frybread.

No wonder men followed Theresa around, Margie thought to herself. I got to learn to make frybread like that.

Michael and Zho Wash moved the table to the middle of the room and pulled the couch and chairs up to the table.

"Ambay wiisinin!" Zho Wash called. "Come and eat!" At the table he began to pray aloud in the old Ojibwe language. At each pause in the prayer, Michael affirmed, "Mm hmm," and nodded. The girls sat quietly: their knowledge of traditional ways and language was limited, and they could understand only an occasional word. At the end of the prayer, when Michael responded, "Hoh," they looked up apologetically.

"What I was saying was this," the old man said kindly, and translated the prayer into English. He had been thanking the Creator for the day, for the food, for all the good things that had been given to us in this world, and for his son and the girls, asking blessings for everyone there and their families, wishing them good lives, he said.

They ate the frybread with the rabbit soup, Theresa (apprehensively nibbling the first small bit of rabbit, said, "It's good!" in obvious relief) and Margie chewing and sipping neatly, the men eating two and three helpings to each girl's one, using their bread to mop up those last puddles of broth in their bowls. Zho Wash had given Margie the bowl that had been his younger wife's favorite, the one with the purple bands around the sides, and the shiny spoon with the handle shaped like a pistol. He watched without looking at the young woman who watched without looking at his son, watched his son turn his head to talk to Theresa, who had risen from her chair to pass the plateful of frybread his way.

For dessert Michael had bought at the Skelly station a can of blueberry pie filling that he heated on the woodstove in the emptied saucepan. When it bubbled he dropped in the last pieces of frybread. "It's like dumplings," he said. "My grandma used to make blueberry stew and cook these little dumplings in it when we were kids. Kind of like this." He hummed as he stirred the pot.

Michael's singing was to Margie as Theresa's frybread making was to Michael. She listened to a wordless tune rise and float over the table, pictured him as an old man, a Chippewa grandfather, with an expanse of belly that pushed its weight down onto his belt and turned his beaded belt buckle nearly upside down. She closed her eyes, and the scene became real. The grandfather who was Michael stirred soup in one pot, turned walleye fillets over in the old cast-iron frying pan that had been his father's, wiped his hands on the ends of the dish towel tucked and folded around his belt. On the other side of the room, Theresa changed a baby's diaper on the couch while little children played on the floor; at the table, older girls helped Margie mix frybread dough and peel carrots. A teenage boy walked in the back door; the front of his jacket was snow-crusted; he held up a rabbit on a snare. His mouth was open, laughing; his smile brilliant as a July sun in the dark cabin; his eyes, nearly closed, were dancing crescents balanced on his high, sharp cheekbones; his teeth strong and white.

Michael spoke. "Sometimes my grandma used to mix blueberries into her frybread," he said. His voice was a young man's, which opened Margie's eyes to the present as well as, finally, what she had been ignoring since he had opened the car door, that his attention was clearly on Theresa, who went to college, on her long black hair, her beauty, her frybread making, the sum of everything that Theresa was and that Margie was not. The tar paper shack, which her grandmother Maggie had probably left for a good reason, was cramped and dark; it smelled faintly of mildew. Michael was smitten by Theresa, who as far as Margie could tell seemed to be casting some kind of spell over him by not appearing to particularly notice or care; toward the old man, Michael's kindly father who had seen it all from the beginning and pitied Margie, she began to feel a faint dislike.

Margie had her pride. She told herself that it didn't hurt, it didn't hurt, it didn't hurt. "What a good idea!" she said a trace too enthusiastically. "I'll have to try that!" Once I learn how to make frybread.

"It turned the dough blue," said Michael. "It sure was good."

"I wonder what else she put into it?" pondered Margie thoughtfully, like a woman with frybread experience and knowledge.

At the bottom of the saucepan a piece of frybread was sticking to scorched pie filling. Michael scraped at it gently, then with more pressure, which caused the slippery purple lump to flip out of the pan and over his shoulder. It landed on one of Zho Wash's moccasins, which was lying sole-up on the floor.

"Ai . . . shtaaa," said Michael.

"I'll take that one," said Zho Wash, politely.

Margie scooped the frybread from the moccasin sole with a dish towel. "Your pretty moccasin." Animatedly, she dabbed at the leather. "Look, it didn't get on the top at all, just the bottom; it won't show at all when you have it on." She placed her hand inside the moccasin to show the old man how it would look upright, just slightly turned away in order to not have to directly see Michael and Theresa. The black velveteen vamp and cuff, trimmed with red ribbon and heavily beaded with Ojibwe-style tendrils and flowers, showed some wear; this wasn't the first pair of moccasins they had decorated. The moose hide sole, wrapped and gathered to the vamp, was new-looking, clean except for the blue stain on the bottom. Who had done that for Zho Wash, carefully detached velvet from worn hide, carefully reattached it to a new moccasin cut and sewn to fit his old foot? "See?" she asked. "Lookit there." She opened her lips, lifted the corners of her mouth, showed her teeth, hoped that it looked like a smile. Remembered the patch of brown decay on the side of her left eyetooth and closed her lips over the grimace.

"That was just lucky, that it was upside down," said Theresa.

"It won't show as long as you dance traditional," said Michael. "Watch." He took the moccasin from Margie, put both his father's moccasins on his own feet, and two-stepped lightly, deliberately, humming a love song. Zho Wash drummed with a wooden spoon on the dishpan, singing in his thinning, old man voice, "I don't care about none of that, sweetheart; I only care about you," and Michael stepped higher, knees raised, shoulders lowered. Getting fancy, he whooped. Indigo blue winked from the stain on his left sole, catching light reflected on the chainsaw from the fluorescent ceiling fixture and Margie's eye. She laughed too loudly, felt Zho Wash notice and considerately ignore it, hated him for it.

~ ~ ~

Back in the car, while Theresa hummed along with the radio, Margie closed her eyes and pretended to be asleep. Somewhere between Sweetgrass and the highway she drifted into a dream country, where in Zho Wash's cabin an old woman mixed with her fingers a lively white dough in a wooden bowl carved from the burl of a maple tree. She looked up at Margie; her face was brown and lined as bark; against the dough her swollen knuckles were dark and crooked shapes.

"*Feels good on old hands, that warm dough,*" the old woman said without words, since in the dream they weren't needed.

"*Frybread, ina?*" Margie asked silently.

"*Lugalette,*" the old woman answered, "*we called it lugalette. We used to bake it in a pan. But lugalette dough makes good frybread, too.*" From a basket on the table she poured blueberries into the bowl, worked them gently into the dough with her fingers, then from a small brown paper sack shook the secret ingredient, the littlest bit of sugar, into the dough. "*Now you try it,*" she said, and with her hands of vapor guided Margie's.

Gently, so gently, because of the tenderness of the old woman's hands, Margie mixed the lugalette dough. Gently, so gently, under the old woman's fingers Margie's hands shaped frybread, delicate hollow ovals that in a black skillet of hot lard turned into thick gold rings studded with sapphires.

The old woman took the first bite, and nodded. "*Mii-gwayak; you did good.*"

The frybread tasted of late summer, blueberries under a warm sun picked by a child; it tasted of hard work, of thick pelts trapped and traded for winter supplies, flour and lard and the luxury of a small sack of sugar; it tasted of the land of dreams, the land of the seen and the land of the unseen; it tasted of magic. "*Jee-bik,*" the word formed back of Margie's lips, and she said it aloud. Hearing herself, she kept her eyes closed, not wanting to wake.

"*Ay-ah, a little magic is a good thing, as is a little secret.*" The old woman's voice was growing distant.

Margie wondered without words.

"*It will be all right.*" The voice had nearly disappeared. "*Come back to Sweetgrass; it is yours, after all. Come back, and take good care of my grandson; take good care of Zho Wash.*"

"Zho Wash?" Margie opened her eyes. The old woman was gone. They were nearly to the Dionne Fork.

"You awake now?" Theresa laughed. "Where you been, my girl? Look, there's that Skelly station. We need to stop for some gas."

"Let's get some coffee, too; I'll buy. And I'll take a turn driving. That was good frybread you made."

"You should try it. If I can make it, you can make it."

Oh, and will Michael watch me the way he watches you? "Well, I'm thinking I might do that."

"So, what did you think of Michael?"

~ ~ ~

Inside the Skelly station an older couple and the girl Michael had called Dale Ann were sitting at a short linoleum-covered counter, the man and woman playing cribbage and the girl reading a paperback book. They looked up, the man beaming and the girl pushing her heavy glasses up her long skinny nose. "Come on in," the woman said pleasantly. "Don't forget to wipe your feet."

They asked for coffee and five dollars' worth of gas. Dale Ann put on a red wool hunting jacket and went out the door to pump, the woman to a wooden worktable in back of the cash register, where she poured coffee from a percolator into two heavy white cups. "It's a little strong," she warned, "been in the pot awhile."

An oily rainbow floated on the liquid onyx of opaque coffee.

"That's fine; we're driving to Duluth and it'll keep us awake," Margie answered.

"Oh, Duluth, is that where you live? What do you do there?"

"I work there; Theresa goes to the college."

The man, who had been studying a history of cribbage scores in the back pages of a ledger, looked up. "Oh, a college girl; good for you. Our little Dale Ann out there, she was at a college too, in Chicago. She lived with some college girls."

"What college did she go to?" Theresa asked.

The woman seemed a little offended at the question. "She didn't go to college; she was living at a college, with some girls who went to college in an apartment," she explained patiently. "She had a job there, a real good job. Now she's back helping us out, me and Father."

The girl came back in, barely opening the door ("Getting cold out there; don't want to let the heat out, darling," the man said) and then closing it quickly, stepping out of a large pair of bunny boots that she left on the rug, and removing her glasses to wipe white ice condensation onto a handkerchief. As she stretched to hang the hunting jacket on a hook by the door, her blouse rode up, exposing a round potbelly the size of a small saucepan. Self-consciously she pulled the blouse down and her sweater across her middle as she ducked behind the counter to the cash register. "It'll be five dollars for the gas and twenty cents for the coffee," she said.

Niizh: Termination Days

Shades of Through the Looking Glass

1970

"HEY, WHAT D'HELL YOU THINK YER DOIN'?" The old woman in the rusty black coat and overshoes had forgotten to latch the stall door in the ladies' room at the Stevens Point bus depot, and the girl ahead of Dale Ann in line had pulled the door wide open. Perched and huddled on the edge of the toilet, she glared at both girls, a crow ruffled and outraged, caged in a public toilet stall. "Get the hell out of my goddam toilet, you."

The girl ahead of Dale Ann blushed. "She didn't lock the door."

"Goddamn door's broke; get the hell away from here!"

Another stall door opened as someone came out, and the blushing girl stepped in. Dale Ann held the door closed from the outside for the old woman, who again said, "Get the hell away from me," when she finished and walked out of the stall.

"Dirty pigs, spying on people in the toilet," the crow muttered. She hadn't flushed the toilet. Dale Ann flushed it with her foot.

The depot in Stevens Point was seven hours into the fourteen-hour bus trip from Duluth to Chicago, and Dale Ann hadn't eaten since her mother put her on the bus three hours before that. She bought a candy bar from the lunch counter and climbed back into breath-scented humidity. In the seat next to hers, empty since Duluth, sat the crow, with a brown grocery sack on her lap.

"I ain't sitting by any Indian," she called to the front of the bus. "She's gonna have to sit by somebody else."

The bus driver walked back and stood in the aisle next to the seat. "Ma'am, you'll have to find yourself another seat, then," he told her. "The young lady doesn't have to move." The old woman rustled her wings angrily but rose and walked up and down the aisle. There was one empty seat, next to a young man who stood and asked if she wanted the window or the aisle.

"Well, I ain't sitting by HIM," she called to the bus driver.

"Why not, ma'am?"

"Well, he's BLACK!"

The young man stood looking evenly at the luggage rack, waiting.

"He can just go sit by HER!"

The bus driver raised his voice. "That's his seat, and that's her seat, and you can sit by him or you can sit by her, or you can get off the bus!"

The young black man pulled his grip from the luggage rack and walked up the aisle to Dale Ann. She nodded her head and he sat, tipping his hat down over his face to sleep. The crow, pleased that she had two seats to herself, set her grocery bag down next to her so hard that an orange bounced up and out, made a thud on the floor, and rolled up the aisle to the front of the bus. She settled, preening, with a creak and flap of her rusty black coat.

As the bus backed out of the parking lot, the young man raised his hat and turned to Dale Ann. "Miss? Are you a real Indian?" She nodded. "My great-grandmother was a full-blooded Seminole Indian princess. She was very proud of that." Dale Ann nodded again, politely, her eyes down. A princess, she sighed to herself.

~ ~ ~

The relocation program worker had come all the way from Minneapolis to County North just to talk to Dale Ann, who was one of two Indian students who had made it to their senior year of high school. She was in her usual place in English class, half-hidden behind Jackie Minogeezhik and watching Mr. Strand over Jackie's beefy right shoulder, when the door opened. Today, as he did every day, Jackie was wearing one of his two white dress shirts, both from the boxes of used clothing regularly sent by the Duluth Catholic Diocese to the St. Francis priest. The ladies of the St. Francis parish's Kateri Circle, who sorted the donations, had alerted Mrs. Minogeezhik to the shirts, big enough in the shoulders for Jack and like new except for a small L-shaped rent in the yoke of one. Every morning Mrs. Minogeezhik washed one shirt by hand in the kitchen sink; every morning she ironed the other shirt that she had hung outside the day before to dry and bleach out in the sun. Seated behind Jackie, Dale Ann listened to the English teacher, took notes, and read, all the while inhaling the comforting scent of the outdoors and Fels-Naptha. Each day she looked to see which shirt he wore, the like-new perfect or the like-new with the neat mend above his right shoulder blade.

Dale Ann usually sat slumped down in her seat just enough to stay out of Mr. Strand's sight yet be able to watch him when she wished to. She didn't want to be where he could see her and then call on her, which was his only real fault, as far as she was concerned. Other than that she liked Mr. Strand. He brought his own books, which were better than the ones in the school library, to class, and kept them lined up along the chalk trays below the blackboards for the students to borrow and take home to read. They could keep them as long as they liked, he said, just so they brought them back. Dale Ann, who had lost the first book she had checked out of the school library in September and wasn't allowed to check out another until she returned it, appreciated Mr. Strand's being so generous with his books and had been careful all year to keep track of them. She had especially liked *On the Beach*, *The High and the Mighty*, *Not as a Stranger*, *The Adventures of*

Cricket Smith. Mr. Strand had asked Dale Ann once if she was planning to go to college. She had beamed at the compliment, cherished it, played it back in her mind from time to time.

Protected and half-hidden behind Jack, she listened as Mr. Strand began to talk about another book he liked, *Brave New World.* Had anyone in the class read it, he wondered, looking around the room. He tiptoed and craned his neck in order to find Dale Ann in back of Jack. Saw her. Knew that she had. She sighed, raised her hand.

Andi, the girl who sat across the aisle, hissed, "Oh, yes, Dale Ann Dionne has read *Brave New World.* Dale Ann Dionne has read every single book in the whole wide world. Brownnoser."

What part of the book did Dale Ann think was the most interesting, asked Mr. Strand. The colonies, she said. What they did with the people who wouldn't fit in. In what way was that their punishment, the teacher asked. She mumbled, knowing from experience that if she continued to mumble he would eventually answer his own questions.

"What was that, Dale Ann?"

Mumble, mumble.

The door was opened by an office cadet, who held it wide for the man in the suit who hesitated, smiling, in the doorway to the classroom until the teacher walked over. They whispered for half a minute, then Mr. Strand announced that Dale Ann Dionne was wanted in the office.

"Ooh, Dale Ann's in trouble now. What did she do, smoke in the bathroom? Steal a car? Read too many books?" The hiss had become audible to the entire room, except for Mr. Strand.

Andi's hair was awfully greasy, and not only at the roots, Dale Ann thought. When was the last time she washed it? It didn't even look blonde, really, except at the ends. She picked up her books and her purse and followed the man in the suit out the door.

"You're not in trouble, Dale Ann. Right, Carol?" he said, as though he and the cadet had been playing a practical joke that he was going to let Dale Ann in on. He was cute, boyish in his suit and tie, his longish dark hair curling over his collar and the sides of his dark-framed glasses. Carol tittered at the private joke shared just between the two of them, shook her head, gushed, "No, Mr. Gunderson, she isn't!" She seated Dale Ann and the man in the suit at the table in the teachers' lunchroom and bounced to the door; her tiny plaid skirt flipped up almost to her underpants with every step.

"Thank you, Carol." He had a pleasant voice, like Andy Williams's.

Her hand on the doorknob, Carol pivoted on the balls of her feet, showing her teeth. Her hair and skirt swung as she spun; her ankles clicked; she nearly saluted. "You're welcome," she sang to the man in the suit, and was gone.

He told Dale Ann that he had come to congratulate her. She had been recommended by her teachers to participate in a special program for American Indian young people who were good students, who showed potential. He, Mr. Gunderson, worked for the federal government and traveled to high schools all over the Upper Midwest to meet those students and to tell them about the federal relocation program.

"Dale Ann, the federal relocation program is looking for young Indian people like you, who have shown in school that they have the ability to succeed in life if they are given the opportunity to do so." Mr. Gunderson had changed from flirty boy to earnest big brother. "Your principal told me that you are a good student, that you will be the first person in your family to graduate from high school. They must be proud of you."

Mumble, mumble.

"Have you thought about what you would like to do after you graduate?"

Should she tell him that Mr. Strand had asked her if she'd thought about college?

"College isn't for everyone, you know." Had he read her mind?

"But there are many opportunities for education and work training out there for a young woman that can lead to a fine future."

The federal government was offering Dale Ann a bus ticket to Chicago and training as a long-distance telephone operator at Illinois Bell. She would have a job with a regular paycheck and would learn a skill that would make her employable for the rest of her life so that she would always be able to find a job; she would be self-sufficient and independent. She would have a relocation worker, someone like Mr. Gunderson, who would look after her, make sure that she knew how to handle her money, how to budget so that she could pay her own bills and even send some money home. "She's a terrific girl, not that much older than you; her name is Miss Novak. I've met her, and we've talked about you. She is looking forward to meeting you. You won't have to worry about anything; she will meet you at the bus depot and get you set up in an apartment; she'll take good care of you and get you on your feet."

How far away was Chicago? "Well, I was thinking of looking for a job around here after graduation."

This was the opportunity of a lifetime, and it would be a shame to waste it, Mr. Gunderson said. Sure, with her high school diploma Dale Ann would have an advantage over a lot of other people, but there really was no opportunity at all on Indian reservations, especially Mozhay Point. Even in town or at the mining company offices, there weren't many jobs available for a girl without any type of training. After all, Dale Ann hadn't taken the office and business training classes. Just typing, wasn't that right?

"Um, yes," Dale Ann answered, mortified at her lack of planning. She had thought typing was fun, but chose Spanish and choir over shorthand and bookkeeping.

"But typing will give you a great background for switchboard work!" She would enjoy the specialized training she would receive to become a long-distance operator; it was detailed, it was demanding, it wouldn't be easy, but Mr. Gunderson had confidence that she would be up to the challenge. "And just think, Dale Ann, what this will mean to your family. Not only will you set an example for the other young people at Mozhay Point, but you can send money home to help." He turned back into cute and flirty Mr. Gunderson. "Why, your sisters could have pretty things; all girls like pretty things, don't they?" And back to Mr. Gunderson the earnest big brother. "This can make the difference to your family; your sisters and your little brother can have a chance at life, and this would all be because of you, Dale Ann. This is an opportunity for you to realize your potential, to make the most of the abilities you have and make a difference in life for yourself and your entire reservation."

The girl began to read through the folder of material on the table.

"There's no future up here for a girl like you. Do you want to waitress, work at a resort? You could do that, but do you really see that for yourself? Life here can be hard, Dale Ann. It can be a hard life here for a girl like you, a girl with your kind of potential. This is the way out, Dale Ann, but it's up to you. The decision is yours."

~ ~ ~

Miss Novak had taken care of everything, just as Mr. Gunderson had said she would. She mailed to Dale Ann, through Mr. Strand, work contracts to sign, an apartment lease, picture postcards of the Hancock Building and the Museum of Science and Industry. She arranged for Dale Ann to see a doctor in Mesabi for a physical examination, a dentist to fill her teeth. She sent a thick envelope of information from Illinois Bell, a map of Chicago and Evanston, the first half of a round-trip Greyhound bus ticket to Chicago (Miss Novak would hold the other half for Dale Ann's visit home at Christmas). She sent Dale Ann her new address and telephone number in Evanston. She would be living with two college girls, who had volunteered to take a reservation Indian girl into their apartment and introduce her to life in the city.

She received a letter from Evanston, a small bright orange envelope bordered with pink and yellow psychedelic daisies. The handwriting was rounded, girlish.

> Dear Dale Ann,
>
> We are so eager to meet you that I thought I would write before your arrival! You know us already as Elizabeth and Catherine, but everyone calls us Buff and Cat. Do you have a nickname?
>
> We have met your friend Miss Novak, and she has brought sheets and blankets for your bed (I have made your bed for you, and my dolls, Tiny Tears and Raggedy Ann, are sleeping there right now!). Miss Novak will be meeting you at the Chicago bus depot and will come with you to the apartment. We will have Dunkin' Donuts and hot chocolate while we get acquainted!
>
> Looking forward to seeing you next Tuesday! This will be such fun!
>
>> Your new roomie and friend,
>> Catherine (Cat)

"Toke?" The young man who lived on the mattress in the corner of the living room looked up, smiling with his beautiful and whole teeth, white as Chiclets, and held out a friendly hand, joint pinched between thumb and forefinger, to Dale Ann as she walked in the front door of the apartment after finishing her three-to-eleven shift at the telephone company. "Toke, Operator?" His voice squeaked with the effort to keep his lungs filled with smoke.

"No, I don't think so, Charles; thanks anyway."

"Dale E-ehn!" Catherine, who Dale Ann had found almost immediately was the nicer of her two roommates, unwound her slender and graceful arms from around Charles's neck and her slender and graceful body from its contorted curl against Charles's back and shoulders, and stood and tottered across the room. She embraced Dale Ann, pressed her cheek against Dale Ann's. Her

skin and hair were warm and fragrant; Dale Ann held still, allowing herself to be stroked and patted, inhaling the damp sweetness
that was Catherine: warm milk and nutmeg, baby powder, the
Cupid's Quiver orange blossom douche packets she used to scent
her underwear drawer. "Dale E-ehn, you feel so cold. Are you
cold? Let me help you." She pulled off Dale Ann's mittens, untied
her scarf, began to unbutton her coat. "She's cold, Charles," she
cooed. "She needs your blanket, she needs coffee. And she needs
M&M's. And licorice." This addressed to the girl seated on the
floor next to her mother's discarded Duncan Phyfe coffee table.
    ". . . of course." Buff, the other roommate, hesitated just long
enough to let Dale Ann know she was out of her place before
she pushed the crystal punch bowl of candy across the floor to
the edge of Charles's mattress, next to the percolator. "Would
you like a piece of candy?" She would not push it directly to
Dale Ann, who she knew couldn't just choose a piece of candy
and eat it but would try to pull Buff into the guilt trip that so
far Buff had managed to avoid. Dale Ann would first carefully
touch the bowl, run her hands along its sides, perhaps comment
on its feel and weight, and just generally reproach Buff with her
poor-me attitude, poor little Indian girl who had to work to pay
rent and couldn't go to any college at all, let alone a school like
Northwestern. Buff was irritated and offended by Dale Ann, who
seemed to think that she had landed in some sort of wonder-
land that was a cross between Buckingham Palace and a country
club (if Dale Ann knew what either was, which Buff doubted):
she admired at length Buff's things, the mismatched china and
crystal brought from home as a joke she didn't get, Buff's purple lace-up boots with the chunky heels, her red Thunderbird,
her debutante ball album, looking and touching as though she
were at a museum or studying for an exam, committing it all to
memory. She read Buff's art history textbook and film encyclo-
pedia while she ate lunch at the kitchen table, after clearing off

the dirty dishes and wiping off crumbs and circles of spilled orange juice, another reproof. Handled everything so annoyingly and overly carefully, washing and drying Buff's mother's Wedgewood plate and cup and her Waterford crystal highball glass as soon as she had finished; she had even said once that she would like to bring a plate home to show to her mother when she visited at Christmas. Buff, of course, had had to tell her that she would not want her to do that, which embarrassed Dale Ann, who had said in her meek and reproachful voice, "oh." Several mornings every week, always different mornings and half the time Saturdays or Sundays, Buff woke to the sounds of Dale Ann getting ready to go to the telephone company for her job. Each time Buff turned on her side and covered her ear with the pillow trying to stay asleep; each time the sounds formed a picture that tormented her: Dale Ann's windup alarm clock clattered tinnily; Dale Ann brushed her teeth, dressed, ate; took her limp, imitation suede coat out of the hallway closet (where she would drape it carefully over a hanger when she got home, in order to try to give it some shape), put it on over one of her cheap-looking work outfits (that she would change out of as soon as she got home), and walked to work to save bus fare. Treated herself to a pair of vinyl shoes, or a hairbrush, or a bottle of drugstore cologne on payday. Lived and breathed in Buff's air, sleeping on a cot in the tiny study, cleaning the bathroom on Saturdays (Buff and Cat never cleaned the bathroom, but Dale Ann never said anything as she scrubbed out the bathtub like a martyr), paying her share of the rent on the first of the month from her checking account, subtracting the amount carefully in the little register, all in a general rebuke, to Buff in particular but to Cat and Charles and all of their friends, too, although Cat couldn't see it. Cat still thought it was simply super ("semp-ly seu-pah") to have what she thought was the exotic presence of an Indian from somewhere out in the woods right there in her and Buff's apartment. Perhaps Cat thought that Dale Ann was an Indian princess who would emerge from her room one day dressed in a feathered headband and leather dress; so far, she had emerged in that pilled flannel nightgown and sweatshirt for bed, or for work in that blue Orlon cardigan over one of her flowered homemade dresses, or her sweater and skirt outfit and those cheap shoes, topped by that imitation suede coat. Outfits as exotic, Buff supposed, as Dale Ann's embarrassingly low-paying, dead-end job with a shift schedule that disrupted the lifestyle of her roommates. Dale Ann was, to put it simply, born to a different way of life; Buff knew it, Dale Ann knew it, and there wasn't any point in their trying to pretend that she wasn't. And Buff thought that Dale Ann looked more Jewish than anything else.

Charles poured a handful of M&Ms into his mouth. "Head food, Operator," he smiled, crunching the sweetness of candy shell and chocolate. "Hey, you know what is a really trippy head food? Omelets. I was going to make omelets, but someone ate all of the eggs."

"It was you, Charles! Don't you remem-bah?" Catherine laughed with delight. "You scrambled an en-TIE-uh dozen and ate them when you got up today!"

That doesn't surprise me, Dale Ann thought. He stayed with Catherine and her roommates for free, slept every day until noon, sat on his mattress drinking coffee and listening to the Moody Blues when he wasn't in class, sold pot for spending money, and ate like a horse. Charles's parents sent him a check at the beginning of every quarter to pay his tuition and another every month for his living expenses. The first he deposited in his checking account that seeded the cash flow of his growing pot business; the others he cashed and gave to the Students for a Democratic Society. "The Movement needs the money more than I do," he explained to Dale Ann one night as he ate the last of the TV dinners she had bought at the A&P.

Her coat off, Dale Ann allowed her rather childlike roommate to embrace her for several seconds, warming herself against Catherine's soft skin, the color of cream, and Catherine's peach-colored satin nightgown, part of Charles's mother's honeymoon trousseau that he had found in a trunk in the basement when he was home for a weekend and given to Catherine for her birthday. Dale Ann thought that Catherine looked like a movie star in Charles's mother's slinky nightgown. Just think, the young woman who wore that gave birth to Charles, she thought to herself. Maybe even conceived him in it. Just think, Charles's mother had been a young woman during the Second World War, and she was probably thinking how lucky it was that her baby would be born during peacetime, and she made sure he took vitamins and got his teeth straightened and went to college, and that there was no chance at all that he would be drafted because that was for somebody else's baby and not hers, and now she thinks he's living at the Deke frat house instead of on a mattress and doesn't have any idea that she is a patron of the SDS.

By the time Dale Ann had put on her nightgown and sweatshirt and poured a bowl of Sugar Pops from the stash of food she kept in her dresser drawer, a secret from Charles, several friends of Catherine's and Buff's had come into the apartment and were sitting on the living room floor. At first she didn't see them but stood in the doorway between the living room and study, saying, "Jeez, it's cold in here; why don't they turn the heat on?" Buff's eyes rolled ceilingward ("NOW what did I say?" thought Dale Ann), and Catherine, by then a little stoned, said in her gracious but rather slowed finishing-school voice, "Dale Ann, I'd like you to meet Janey, and Paul, and Button, and Tracy, and James, and Brian. This is our new roommate, Dale Ann."

James actually stood and said, "It's a pleasure to meet you, Dale Ann."

Was he waiting to shake her hand? She said, "You, too," and held her hand out. He didn't pump it up and down, but held it for just a second, lightly, before he let go. Buff rolled her eyes again.

Dale Ann said, "Hi," to the rest of the room, conscious that she was the only one there in a flannel nightgown and sweatshirt. Was this a party? Was she invited? Should she go to bed?

"Sit with us, Operator?" There was plenty of space next to Charles on the mattress; Catherine's body, thin and curled, took up as much space as would a ten-year-old's. "Cat, are there any more graham crackers?"

Catherine once again unwound herself from Charles and stood, put her arms around Dale Ann, more slowly this time and with a trace of a tremor and sway. She must have felt the chill in the room, too, Dale Ann noticed; she was wearing Charles's chambray work shirt over her unsettlingly small shoulders. "Sit here with us, Dale Ann," she said, and with her arm around Dale Ann's waist led her to the mattress on the floor.

"Cat, can you find any more graham crackers?" Catherine's leap was light and in slow motion over the legs on the floor and into the kitchen, slightly off-balance when she came back out with the box of graham crackers. She smiled over Charles's shoulder at Dale Ann as she wound and coiled herself once again at his back. Charles bent a stale cracker in half and pushed the entire thing into his mouth and chewed, lips closed. Swallowed before he spoke. "Toke, Operator? Have you tried it?"

"Why does he call you 'Operator'?" asked one of the girls, a blonde in dirty jeans and an embroidered gauze shirt. She appeared to be preparing to smoke a toilet paper roll. Her eyes crossed as she brought one end closer to her face.

What in the world is she doing, wondered Dale Ann. "Because that's what I do at work; I'm an operator. A telephone operator."

Buff and the blonde looked embarrassed; the blonde lit a small yellow-gray block of hashish with a match, placed the hash in the middle of the toilet paper roll, placed the roll over her mouth, blocked the other end with her hand, gasped, then pulled her hand away. She gagged and coughed, bent so that her face was almost to her knees.

"Shades of Workers of the World!" said one of the boys who, stifling a belch as he took the cardboard roll from the blonde's hand, brushed at the front of his army surplus fatigue jacket, where a spark had landed. "What did she say she is? I thought you said she was an Indian." The first boy said, "She's an Indian? Like Pocahontas? Far out!" The room stared at Dale Ann, too polite to say their collective thought, too stoned to control their collective body language: she doesn't look like an Indian. What is she wearing? Where are her braids? The blonde in the gauze peasant blouse tittered and wheezed.

Then Dale Ann was forgotten. The group talked about their classes, their professors, the antiwar protest planned for Friday afternoon in front of the library. About the Movement. The People. Liberation. James was going to fly to Montreal, then south to illegally enter Cuba to spend spring break with Venceremos, cutting sugarcane in the fields with the workers by day and studying with the revolutionaries by night. "When the Revolution comes the People are going to control things. The workers are key to this, the workers of the world, and that's where the revolution is going to come from. It's going to start with the workers and the students, and we'll be joined by everyone else, the Black Panthers and everyone else who has been downtrodden. The whole Establishment, the corporations and the pigs and fascists are going to have to run for their lives. That's what the Movement is all about. Power to the people."

"Right on," choked one of the girls, who had been passed the toilet paper roll.

Buff's voice sounded squeezed, as though her lungs were clenched in a large fist. "I told my dad that the Revolution is coming." She exhaled a cloud of smoke. "I told him that he should get rid of his stocks and his investments before it happens, before he loses everything. I needed to tell him; he is my father, after all."

"Stocks and investments support the war machine. Get rid of them. Like this." The baby-faced boy dug into the punch bowl and crammed a handful of M&Ms into his mouth. He chewed and swallowed. "Did you see that? Get rid of them. Chew them up, swallow them. Get rid of them," he said, and began to laugh uncontrollably.

"Can't handle it?" Charles asked sympathetically. "Good shit."

"Shit them out!" the boy guffawed, pounding his fist on his thigh.

"This is serious," Buff said coldly. The laughing boy sat up straight and pressed a sofa pillow against his mouth. His eyes watered; he snorted and coughed; his shoulders shook.

"It is not funny. The people dying on the other side of the world will be our brothers and sisters in revolution."

The boy howled into the pillow.

"Brian." Charles said it quietly. "Cool it."

"Do you want the pigs here, the police, the fuzz, man?" James's words sounded humorous to Dale Ann, spoken in an accent like her father's hero, the dead President Kennedy, but they had an effect on Brian, who stopped laughing and jumped up to check at each of the three front windows. He looked up, down, side to side, through each. "Nobody out there, man," he said, and pulled down the shades.

"The Revolution is going to break this country's military forces right in half," said James. "It will separate the baby killers from the soldiers who were drafted, who are Nixon's victims like the other workers who are held in captivity all over the world."

"It'll separate the captive workers from the rednecks who support the Establishment, the Pigs."

"The baby killers and the rednecks and the entire military-industrial complex are going to have to run for their lives, too. We're pacifists, but we won't be able to keep that from happening."

"The Revolution is the only thing that's going to end the war; it's the only way to give peace a chance."

One of the boys licked his thumb and forefinger, and shot an M&M from between them at the blonde, who giggled, "Paul, don't be juvenile," and shot one back.

Buff became tearful. "When I told my father what he needs to do before the Revolution comes, he didn't believe me. He laughed at me. Then he told me that if he finds out from ANYWHERE, from the six o'clock news, or sees my picture in the newspaper, or someone who sees me tells him, that I'm anywhere NEAR an antiwar demonstration, he'll stop my tuition and my living allowance and my rent. He said he'll have me sent home so fast that I won't know what happened." She passed the back of her hand delicately under her teary nose. "So I won't be able to go to the library on Friday for the demonstration. Or for the teach-in. He really means it."

"Bummer, Buff."

"Parent shit. What a downer."

"It's as though he thinks he owns everything, including me; it's as though he thinks he can buy anything he wants."

Cat patted Buff's hand, right where she had been wiping her nose, Dale Ann thought, and murmured, whispering, consoling, touching the edge of Charles's work shirt to the edges of Buff's damp eyes, smoothing her hair.

The gathering turned its attention to a more pressing subject.

". . . just stood there, looking at us. He didn't even say anything when he answered the door, and Scott said, hey man, is Cary here? We're here to pick up a lid he has for us. Then this creep, Cary's roommate, said, I'm sorry, we're using all our lids on our pots!" The blonde was indignant.

Laughter. "Maybe he didn't know what you meant!"

"Oh, he knew what Scott meant. How could Cary's room-mate NOT know? Anyway, the problem is, we didn't get the lid."

"Charles, where do you keep your stash?" Paul's grin was wide and loose; his eyebrows raised and lowered suggestively. "Got any for the party?"

Charles, who never gave away the merchandise, became the pleasantly businesslike, long-haired, fringe-vested version of the Charles of a quarter century to the future, who would negotiate property transactions that would support his good-looking family in the gated community of Dakota Hills in the far western sub-urbs of Minneapolis, Minnesota. "Ten dollars will get you a lid tonight, Paulie."

"Scott charges seven, man."

"Ten dollars." Charles's smile was friendly, confident. He would not become the middle-aged Charles whose four sons, hockey stars all, would be driven to practices and games in an SUV the size of some third world houses by their energetic and fit, devoted, and above all competent mother, and who would live in the largest house in his cul-de-sac, if he couldn't drive a simple business deal. "The offer is good all night."

"Who's got bread?" Paul looked around the room at the group, who were all suddenly focused on immediate, and other, needs. Button went into the bathroom; Buff offered the bowl of candy to everyone left in the room, even Dale Ann. The boys began to sing a song they had learned at the frat house, "Far above a Pi Phi's garter, far above her knee . . ."

Paul shrugged. "No bread, man."

"The offer will be good all night, gentlemen."

Paul reached into the punch bowl at the same time as that new roommate Cat and Buff had found through the housing place-ment list. Dale Ann, the operator. She had a job, right?

"Operator. We both seem to like licorice." He asked her about herself, getting short responses but not much else.

Northern Minnesota.

Chicago is pretty big.

Evanston is pretty.

Lake Michigan made her think of Lake Superior and Minnesota.

Forty hours a week. Split shifts or afternoons. Split shifts? Eight to noon and four to eight; afternoons were three to eleven. Payday was every other Wednesday.

"How would you like to buy a lid from Charles for the party?" His grin grew wider and looser; he looked suggestively at her, she thought, from eyes with drooping lids. His eyebrows wiggled; was he flirting with her?

She cleared her throat and stood up, careful to keep her knees and legs covered by her nightgown. "Be right back," she explained, and went into her bedroom, the study, closing the door. She had felt Paul's eyes pass across her back, down to her backside, felt him compare to the white girls in the room the breadth and heaviness of her shoulders, the lankness of her hair; thinking of Cat's light springing walk and of the blonde girl's lazy and careless grace, she felt clumsy, heavy-footed. She was suddenly homesick for Jack; at school she had wondered if he knew how she loved the scent of his shirts, had wondered if perhaps he watched her sometimes, too, when she wasn't looking. Standing in front of him in the line to board the school bus she would sense the warmth of the sun or perhaps his hand, callused and roughened, tenderly stroking her hair, though when she turned, his hands were in his jacket pockets. The day she took his picture sitting on the porch stairs at the old LaForce house on the allotment, she had stepped closer, closer, leaned back and to one side trying to center him in the picture and felt the soft air of summer or perhaps his hand, work-toughened and clumsy, tender on her back, on her arm, the side of her face, though he sat with his elbows on his knees, his hands folded lightly, fingers laced, between them.

After graduation Jack enlisted in the Army. Dale Ann waited

with him, along with her father and Mrs. Minogeezhik, in front of Tuomela's gas station for the Greyhound that he would take to Duluth, to Minneapolis, to Kansas City, to Biloxi. When the bus pulled up, Jack kissed his mother, shook Roy Dionne's hand, and took a long look toward Sweetgrass before he boarded. From the top step inside the bus, he called to Dale Ann, "Don't do anything I wouldn't do!" then took the window seat across the aisle from the bus driver. That day was midsummer; the bus she took to Chicago in the fall might have been the same one, she thought, and she chose the same seat as Jack had.

The study actually had a view, rare in that part of Evanston, of a vacant lot with two skeletal trees. It was a nice room, Dale Ann had thought when her new roommates had shown it to her, as large as the front room at home. Its drawback was that it connected to the apartment's living room by a glass-paned door, which didn't block the sounds of Cat's and Buff's music and socializing. It was hard to get to sleep at night, hard to get up mornings. She turned on the light, pulled the curtain across the glass, and opened the top dresser drawer.

Dale Ann kept her cash folded in a handkerchief that she pinned inside a panty girdle. Taking out a ten-dollar bill, she turned it over, folded it lengthwise, smoothed it, smelled its money scent of woven paper and coins. What would ten dollars buy beyond an ounce of marijuana? An opening of the door and a look inside, then perhaps a step. She might become like them, casual and detached, knowing the inside jokes, knowing the right thing to say. Her words might not draw a glare from Buff, might not stop the room cold. She might become tall and slender, a blonde, green-iris-eyed Dale Ann in bell-bottom jeans and a gauze peasant blouse embroidered with leaves and flowers that looked like the beadwork on velvet some of the old ladies did at Mozhay Point. She might become a blue-eyed, auburn-haired Dale Ann sitting on the living room floor Indian-style, as her first-grade teacher had called it, looking mysterious in an imported eastern caftan, leaning against the couch with her head tipped back, her eyes looking out at the world with that faraway, ethereal, pensive, blue-iris white-girl mystery while she held inhaled smoke deep in her lungs as long as she could and then expelled it without coughing. She might become Dale Ann generously buying a lid of marijuana for her new friends, who surrounded her with the laughter and drawling jargon she understood because she was one of them. "Shades of Sigmund Freud!" "Just play it heavy." "That is SO bourgeois." "See you at the quad this afternoon? Far out." "It was SUCH a head trip!"

She earned ten dollars for every six hours on the switchboard. She had new shoes, she thought, and thirty dollars more in the panty girdle. Sixty dollars in the relocation program's bank account, taken out of her paychecks and deposited jointly to Dale Ann and Miss Novak. Had just sent ten dollars home. She could afford this. Again she folded the bill lengthwise, smoothed it. Smelled again its money scent of greasy coins and woven paper, sweat from people's palms.

There was an envelope on the top of the dresser; she hadn't noticed it earlier. It was addressed in uneven handwriting, pressed thick and dark into the paper by a heavily gripped pencil, mailed to Dale Ann at her Dionne Fork address, then forwarded in her mother's slanting handwriting to Evanston, Illinois.

The letter from Jack smelled musty and old, though it was dated just a month before.

Dear Dale Ann,

You must be in Chicago now. Different from Mozhay I bet. How do you like your job? I am doing ok here. It is pretty hot— we all have suntans. They tell us it will be rainy season pretty soon. The Joes call this place Indian Country, guess they never been to Mozhay! Food is ok. There's some other guys from Minnesota here. Know what they call me? Tecumseh.

The people here are really small. Some are smaller than you! There is an old lady they call her Mama-san, who comes here to sell things. I bought you a present, but it is a surprise. You will just have to see. All right, it's a ring.

Did you hear my cousin had a boy. He will be pretty big by the time I come back.

I showed your picture to Roger, this buddy of mine. He says to tell you, you look like Yoko Ono.

I am writing to you about something pretty important. Hope you will think about this. I wanted to ask but we were both leaving you to Chicago and me to Basic. But I wanted to ask you. I was thinking, maybe we could get married. When I get back. What do you think? That is the ring I bought.

Your the best girl I know, the smartest that's for sure. And a lot prettier than Yoko Ono. Ha, ha! But I mean it. And you know that, right?

Please write back.

> Your True Love, whether we get married or not,
> Jack
> p.s. You are the only one for me. Am I the only one for you?

Dale Ann imagined her mother, dying to know what was inside, holding the envelope flat on the palm of her hand as though the words might sink and fall through the paper onto her skin. Grace would have perhaps held it up to the kitchen light fixture, that O-ring of ghostly blue fluorescence, clicked her tongue in disappointment at the thickness of the paper, considered telephoning Dale Ann to ask if she would like to have it opened and read to her, decided against the idea because of the expense of a long-distance call. Instead, she would have opened the kitchen cupboard to copy Dale Ann's address from where she had written it on the back of the door onto the envelope. Her pen she kept on the top shelf inside the cupboard, next to the large mayonnaise jar in which she stored the First Communion veil, worn by Dale

Ann and then her sisters Yvonne, Annette, and Cecile, to protect it from mildew and yellowing.

Dale Ann didn't know that after writing "please forward" and her Evanston address on the letter, Grace took down the jar and cradled it in her arms for a minute, as tenderly as she had held Dale Ann as a baby girl, picturing Dale Ann's First Communion, the stubborn straightness of her dark hair temporarily conquered by dampened pin curls X'd into Dale Ann's scalp the night before.

She looked around the room for a piece of paper; finding none, she picked up a paperback copy of *Franny and Zooey*, rescued from Buff's wastebasket, and tore the last, blank page from the back. She sat on her bed and began to write

Dear Jack

Knuckles rapping against glass, Paul's voice crooning against the door. "Dale Ann? Dale Ann, could I come in?"

She moved the curtain, saw Paul's cheek pressed against the window, surrounded by steam from the heat of his skin against glass. He turned his face toward her, his forehead smearing the glass.

"Could I come in, Dale Ann?"

She folded the page in half, inserted it back into the book, and opened the door. He closed it behind him, sat on the cot. Pulled off his Dingo boots, dropped them heavily on the floor. Lay back on her new bedspread from India, bought last payday. His feet smelled unwashed, damp. I'll have to air out the bedspread, she thought.

He lay on the cot, hands knotted back of his neck, looking around the room. "Nice window," he commented. "Nice room. And you have it all to yourself. At the House we have to have roommates; we don't get single rooms until we're seniors." The girl mumbled, hmm, and rearranged the vase, the bottle of cologne, the hairbrush on the top of the chest of drawers. Centered a small pile of photographs onto the cover of a *Mademoiselle* magazine.

"What's your sign, Dale Ann?"

She turned, mumbled. Paul was red, she thought. His skin was rosy, his hair blond ringlets, the photo negative of Dale Ann's pin-curled hair in the snapshot of her First Communion day that Grace kept with the veil in the jar. Wiry blonde hair curled out from the deep pink of his forearms. He looked flushed, overheated, lying on her bed with hands knotted back of his neck, looking around the room, cooling his damp feet and sweat-dampened armpits in the draft that came in through the top of the window, where it didn't quite shut.

"Can I see your pictures?"

She handed him the neatened and squared stack.

"Who are these people? Is this your family?" As he flipped through the pile, she identified them. My mother and dad, Aunt Lisette. Those are some of my aunts and uncles. My sister Cecile; that's her dress she made in school."

"Who's this?" Cousin Butchie, winding up for a pretend pitch at Uncle Biik's house in Duluth. Butch clowning, exaggerating every move. Butch, a scarecrow in his father's old work pants and a white T-shirt that was shrunken in length and stretched in width.

"My older cousin; that's Butch kidding around."

"And who is this?" Jack in his school clothes, ironed white dress shirt and creased wash pants, sitting on the porch at Zho Wash's cabin, on the old LaForce allotment land. His elbows rested on his knees, his hands were clasped. He smiled with his lips closed, the corners of his mouth crimping as he tried not to laugh at Michael Washington, who stepped closer, closer, making faces in back of Dale Ann, who squinted through the viewfinder of the Instamatic camera that Roy and Grace gave her for graduation.

"A boy from home."

"H.T.H.?"

"What?"

"Home-town honey. Your boyfriend back at home?"

Mumble.

"What's he doing with his mouth? Kidding around?"

"Well, no; he's missing a tooth in front."

Paul looked embarrassed to know somebody who had a friend who was missing a tooth in front, but remembered his manners, it seemed. "Nice pictures, Dale Ann. Thank you for letting me see them." *Where did she keep her money?* He put the photographs neatly back on the *Mademoiselle* and pivoted to face Dale Ann, leaning toward the wall with one hand on each side of her shoulders, his breath wet and smelling like strawberry licorice. He had grown redder and warmer, it seemed. He lowered one arm, stroked Dale Ann's face with a sticky hand, large and damp, like his feet. His other armpit, sweat-soaked, was inches from her face. She ducked, shifted to one side. He pinned her to the wall, armpit heavy on her shoulder, passed his other hand across her lower abdomen, up to her waist, pausing to feel through her flannel nightgown the waistband of her underpants, up her side to her breast, which he squeezed, then to her jaw, which he held between his thumb and fingers. He kissed her, his lips cooler than his face and the inside of his mouth surprisingly lush and sweet. Dale Ann thought of ripe strawberries in August, paused, considered; then Paul slipped his fingers between her lips and teeth and onto her tongue. They tasted of salt and smelled faintly of urine. She turned her head, wiped her mouth. He squeezed her jaw, forced his thumb past her teeth to the roof of her mouth. She gagged, bit. He wiped his hand on his shirt, and she thought he might be pulling back to hit her; instead, he gripped her nightgown and backed her up to the edge of the cot. He pushed with his hands, then his stomach and chest; she fell flat on her back, weighted by Paul's body from her knees to her chest.

"Not a sound," he whispered. "Not one sound."

She felt cold metal, the zipper on his fly cutting sharp designs on her skin, pictured a butter knife with small teeth. Over Paul's shoulder the light fixture, shaped like a white-glass cupcake paper, was dotted with dead trapped flies.

Dale Ann stared the light fixture into snow that covered like a white lace handkerchief the ground outside the LaForce family's old cabin on the allotment, stepped on by a doe, cautiously at first, then confidently and unwisely, because the doe had walked into one of Joe Washington's snares and hung there with front hooves dangling, bleeding into the snow. She kept the picture and played it for Paul with eyes that were dry and unblinking until he pulled her nightgown back down over her thighs and rolled on one elbow to breathe on her face.

"You know you wanted it," he said, and stood. He picked up the ten-dollar bill that she had dropped onto the floor.

She didn't make a sound.

"I did you a favor," he said as he opened the door into the living room. He closed it behind him, leaving Dale Ann in the study.

"She's not my type," he said to the group.

"Her face reminds me of a seal," he said to Charles.

"Frigid," he said to Brian.

Catherine knocked on the study door. "Dale Ann? Dale Ann, is everything all right?"

"Everything's fine," Dale Ann answered. "I need to get to bed; got to work in the morning."

~ ~ ~

Dale Ann decided to leave the bedspread and the vase, and packed everything else into her suitcase and a laundry bag, leaving her key to the apartment on the cot with a note, "Cat and Buff, thanks for everything." Listening at the study door until she heard nothing but voices that seemed to come from the other end of the apartment, she picked up the suitcase and bag, turned the doorknob. When she opened the door and looked into the living room only the blonde and James remained, the boy lying on the floor in front of the couch with eyes closed and head back, the girl straddling his lap. She stared without speaking at Dale Ann crossing the floor and going out the front door.

~ ~ ~

Dale Ann took the El to downtown Chicago, walked to the Greyhound station, bought a ticket, and waited through the night in a contoured, scooped-out seat of one of the yellow plastic benches. The fluorescent lights turned her hands a green-tinged yellow that was darker and less lively than the benches. Across the aisle two young black men in identical Afro haircuts sat side by side, in matching white shirts and red sweatpants; each crossed his legs, right over left, and jiggled one foot. Both wore high-topped black tennis shoes; the bottoms of the shoes were new-looking, white.

When the Greyhound driver opened the bus door, Dale Ann was waiting at the front of the line. Again, as she had on the ride from Mozhay to Chicago, she sat across from the driver, in the front row, from where she would see the Dionne house as the bus drove up to the Skelly station and perhaps avoid Grace or any sisters who might be outside. The last passenger on was a young woman who had stayed at the end of the line, allowing passenger after passenger ahead of her, leaning into the chest of the young man who embraced her. They showed no sign of moving. "Got to get going, miss," the driver told her. The man kissed her; she turned, and Dale Ann saw that she held an infant. A diaper bag hung heavily from her shoulder. The young man kissed her face and then the baby's, once more, and watched as the driver helped her up the steps. The man next to Dale Ann stood and offered the girl his seat. There were empty rows in the back where he could sit, he said, and the front row would give her more legroom.

The young mother and the man outside watched each other as the bus driver closed the door and as the bus backed up and left the depot. Then she took several deep breaths, jiggled the infant, and clicked her tongue. "That's my husband I just left there," she told Dale Ann. "He's going to Vietnam." She looked haggard. "My baby is just three weeks old. We're going back to Medford to stay with my family until he gets back." She sat straight up and held the baby tightly, her back not touching the seat. "I was in Chicago a week to see him. He's gonna be there for more than a year. Davey is only three weeks old. He won't even remember this." Her breath was ragged, though her eyes were dry. Dale Ann offered to hold the baby while she settled her things.

"Here, he likes it when you hold him up like this. He's awake; see how he likes to look around? He's gonna be hungry pretty soon; I'll have to nurse him." She stood to push the diaper bag into the luggage rack and sat down and slumped, finally, staring out the front window at the underground streets of Chicago being eaten by the bus taking her away from her husband. Dale Ann held little Davey up the way he liked, wrapped so tightly in his receiving blanket that his body felt stiff and straight. "You can turn him to look at you; he likes that, too," said the girl. "Look at him stare at you! Davey, where's your manners?" The baby rolled his wobbly blue eyes toward his mother, then back to Dale Ann. The girls laughed.

"What's your name? I'm Sharon."

"Dale Ann."

"That's different; I never heard that name before. It has a nice sound."

"Well, it's after my dad, but his name isn't Dale; it's Roy. See, his name is Roy and he really likes Roy Rogers, so they named me after Roy Rogers's wife. You know, Dale Evans?"

"If they like him THAT much, they could have just named you after Roy Rogers—but then you'd have a boy's name."

"Or Trigger has a nice sound to it, too, but then I'd have a horse's name."

They laughed. Dale Ann opened a Three Musketeers bar, broke it in half, and wrapped each half in the paper to keep their hands clean.

"Umm, I feel like I might not be able to keep this down," Sharon apologized. "I haven't been able to eat since yesterday."

"Just do it real slow, in little bites; that'll help you get your appetite back." The girls chewed little bits of the candy bar.

"It's good, thanks. I love Three Musketeers." And Sharon's mouth puckered as if she were trying to hold back a laugh; then it opened and her eyes puckered shut, and she sobbed twice, silently.

"I know a boy who's in Vietnam."

"Is he your husband?" Sharon had a tear left; small, salty-looking, drying as she cried it.

"No . . . Davey looks hungry; here, I think he wants his mom." She handed the baby back to Sharon, who modestly covered her breast and her baby's head with a diaper she pulled from her jacket pocket. She fussed with her bra; Davey turned his face toward her, squirmed, and rooted insistently as he sought her breast. When he found it and clamped on, she winced.

"Does that hurt?"

"Only for a second; in the hospital they told me it gets easier. I hope they're right! There, everything's in place." She took the diaper off the baby's face. He gazed at his mother without blinking, his jaw working up and down, growling with love. The girls laughed again at the tiny man.

"His eyes are so blue," said Dale Ann. "So pretty."

"He's got eyes like his dad," answered Sharon. "Where did that man who was sitting next to you go? It was nice of him to give me his seat. On the way down here to meet Tom I had to stand almost the whole time from Medford to Chicago, holding my baby. Nobody gave up their seat. Nobody even looked at me."

"That's a long time to stand holding a baby and a bag full of stuff."

"Good thing I'm nursing, so I didn't have to worry about bottles and formula. I just had to put our clothes and Davey's diapers in the bag, so it's not that heavy." She hummed to Davey. Dale Ann heard "Happy Together" and "There's a Place for Us"; then Sharon fell asleep feeding her baby. Dale Ann watched the road taking her ever closer to home and Sharon ever farther away from her husband.

~ ~ ~

In Milwaukee, Sharon and her baby slept while half the bus emptied. A young soldier in an army uniform stepped to the door and handed the driver his ticket. The driver asked, "All the way to Duluth?"

"Duluth."

"Going home?"

The soldier nodded and walked up the steps. He stood still for a moment in the aisle next to Sharon and the baby, like an animal that watched and waited before venturing from the woods. He was looking for a place to sit. His eyes were pale, nearly transparent; beautiful they were, Dale Ann thought at first, eyes lighter than the sky, almost white against the sunburned skin of his face. Then she thought that his eyes looked sunburned, too. The soldier walked to the back of the bus and sat in the last row of three empty seats next to the bathroom, his arms around his duffle bag that he held on his lap like Sharon held Davey. He had pretended to ignore the gauntlet, the rows of passengers who stared at, or looked away from, his uniform, and the young couple who appeared outraged that he had boarded the bus. Dale Ann, turning to watch him from behind the tall back of her bus seat, saw that he looked straight ahead, right down the aisle of the bus; he stared beyond the confines of the bus with those sunburned eyes, lighter than the sky and nearly transparent. Dale Ann thought of Uncle Earl's story about the hot blue fires of hell.

Half an hour north of Milwaukee it started to snow, huge flakes that fell faster and faster in a pattern so familiar in its randomness that it became hypnotic. Dale Ann's consciousness drifted with the snow blowing along the side of the highway, but she fought sleep, fearful that she might dream. Cartwheeling from the sky, the flakes grew into spike-studded wheels of ice that spun toward her face and gave her a sudden and unexplainable near panic. She shook her head. I've got to get up and move, she thought; I'll walk back to the bathroom.

Next to the bathroom, the soldier and the man who had given his seat up to Sharon were playing cards over the duffle bag, which lay on the seat between them. The man was talking softly, the soldier listening, his attention not on the cards but far away, mesmerized by sights branded onto the backs of his eyes. The man's voice, pitched just above a whisper, fell gently over the boy's shoulders; calmly and tenderly the soft cadence smoothed and caressed without touching the young soldier, at whom Dale Ann stared from the periphery as she passed.

When she came out of the bathroom, the outraged couple was waiting to go in, the young woman leaning as far as she could from the solder in order to avoid the offense of a passing touch. The soldier's unnerving eyes were down; one hand rearranged his cards, the other held them steadily. The top of his head, with that army haircut so short that his suntanned scalp shone through his dry brown hair, contrasted with the long, leather-bound pigtail worn by the young woman's boyfriend; the soldier looked exposed, in need of cover. Stepping around the seething couple, Dale Ann felt those scorched-blue transparencies blindly brush across her face; turning, she half-smiled at the soldier, who returned to the earth and half-smiled back.

Back in her seat, she took *Franny and Zooey* from her purse and opened the book to the last page, her favorite. It occurred to her that intense and hard to take though Zooey might be, his words, when read slowly, brought Zho Washington to mind. She looked back at the shadowed card game in the back row and at the simmering couple who, back in their seats, complained to one another about the chemical smell of the toilet. Back at the middle-aged woman in the seat behind her, who was knitting a sock under the reading light. She looked down at the page and imagined Jack, who loved cold weather and snow, somewhere in the steamy heat of Vietnam. Kind, silly Cat. Unhappy Buff. The crow at the Stevens Point Greyhound stop.

"What are you reading?" Sharon was awake. "Is it good?"

"It's a story from the fifties. It's a good book."

"Are you a teacher?"

"No, I just like to read."

"Oh. I thought you looked like a teacher. You could be one."

Sharon got off at Medford. "There's my dad," she said as the bus pulled up to the curb in front of a hardware store. Under the weight of the baby and the diaper bag, she stepped down heavily; her father looked into her face for a second and took the bag from her shoulder. She followed him, carrying Davey. Dale Ann wiped steam from the window to watch them walk to a rusting white pickup truck. A dog, long-haired, sloppy, and happy, was waiting in the cab for Sharon; when her father opened the door she patted its muzzle, bent and spoke into its frowsy ear.

With the front seat to herself, Dale Ann put her feet up and watched the snow that came down now in clumps of flakes, like gypsy moths in summer. She took Jack's letter from her purse and reread it by the fading light of early winter and pale green and orange light from the speedometer on the dashboard, tinting the white pages that lay against her knees. She lifted it closer to her face, pondering the musty paper and uneven handwriting brought together by Jack, who sat and wrote somewhere on the other side of the world, where it was damp enough to start mildew in a letter by the time he sealed the envelope. She inhaled until she smelled through the letter's mustiness a faint smoke of cedar, cigarettes, and tanned hide. She reopened the book, reread the last written page, read the beginning of her reply,

Dear Jack

and refolded the paper in half, placed it back inside the book, and turned her head to watch the snow that fell harder and harder, creating deep drifts that the bus bucked along its way up the highway. Mesmerized by the blowing snow and the rocking of the bus, she slept without dreaming until, as the bus pulled into the Duluth Greyhound station, the soldier carried his duffle bag past Dale Ann, the girl who had half-smiled earlier and was now snoring lightly, curled up in sleep with her head resting against the armrest. In the large window that overlooked the terminal, a girl in a quilted ski jacket waved with both arms at the soldier, who was the first passenger through the door. In the seconds that it took for him to reach the sidewalk, she had flown down the stairs so rapidly that his first step onto the concrete of home was also into her arms.

"Welcome home," she whispered, her breath a cloud of steam against his sunburned ear. "Welcome home."

~ ~ ~

North of Duluth, as the cold red winter sun finally set into a long night, Dale Ann woke and switched on the overhead light, reopened *Franny and Zooey*, and began to read it again from the beginning. Finding what was surely fleeting refuge in beautiful Franny's crisis, in the careless comforts of the Glass family's

New York apartment, she avoided looking out the window until the bus slowed, approaching the Skelly station at the fork where the reservation road snaked off toward Sweetgrass. As Dale Ann snapped off the overhead, across the road Grace paused while stuffing a paper garbage bag into the galvanized aluminum trash can next to the front stairs and raised one hand to shield her eyes from the light of the Skelly sign as she peered to see who might be getting off the bus.

The Veil in the Jar

1971

THE FIRST TIME I SAW MARGIE was when she and her friend Theresa stopped at Tuomela's for gas. I went out to pump five dollars' worth; when I came back inside, cold air blew across the counter where they sat drinking coffee. They turned and looked at me over their coffee cups, the tall one sliding those wrap-around almond eyes my way and the other one holding her cup with both hands, her worried-looking mouth open to a little "o" and her eyes murky and iridescently oily as the coffee, and that is how they got an eyeful of my belly when I hung up my coat. They looked like they were glad they weren't me, and the truth is I would have given just about anything to have been one of them and not myself, Dale Ann, my name that had become to me synonymous with the darkness of pain and failure. And betrayal. My life might have turned out differently if I had been one of those pretty girls, one of the girls like Margie and Theresa, sitting there in bell-bottom jeans and their eyes all black-rimmed with eyeliner and chattering about school and jobs and apartments.

The next time was almost two years later, when my mother and I drove to the LaForce cabin with a bagful of cloth diapers (dug out of a box in the closet by Grace, who never threw anything away) for Beryl Duhlebon's poor niece, "that Margie Robineau, who was hanging around with that Michael Washington, and sure enough she got herself in trouble," who had just had a baby. Grace told me that the girl had been abandoned by Michael and refused to leave Zho Washington's house. On top of that, the pitiful disgraced thing needed more than just Cecile's old diapers: in order to keep the county at bay the old man had claimed that the baby was his, but the county's visiting nurse was expected back within the week with a list of baby supplies and household specifications that Zho, Beryl, and Margie were going to have difficulty coming up with. Grace and I were going to help: along with the diapers we were bringing three bars of Ivory soap, a spray can of Lysol, a four-roll pack of toilet paper, a box of prunes, and a bottle of rubbing alcohol, all neatly packed into Grace's Tupperware bread box, the most generous gift of all. In my mother's purse were also a small crucifix for over the baby's bed and a Miraculous Medal for Margie. We were ready to lend a hand and, incidentally, to see who the baby looked like: Michael Washington or, just possibly, his father.

My mother, who never got used to the Mozhay custom of walking right into people's houses, frowned at me when I opened the door to the LaForce cabin. To announce our presence she rapped loudly on the door frame as I whispered "Margie?" to the girl who was humming softly to the baby that slept in her arms.

Margie startled at Grace's knock (only the sheriff and social workers knocked at Mozhay in those days) and rose to her feet. "Auntie Grace!" Flustered, she smoothed her hair and handed the tiny scrap of lavender-pink skin and bones wrapped in one of Beryl's afghans, this one variegated rose-and-coral zigzags that unsettled the eyes, to my mother, and the little thing began to wail miserably.

"Here, Dale Ann, hand that stuff to Margie and you can take the baby," Grace ordered me, as was her habit then and still is today when addressing any of her daughters. Although I was continually working to break the habit of jumping to her orders,

I found that I had been starving to touch an infant and obeyed; I accepted the bundle and Crystal quieted. Her eyes opened and tracked, crossed, tracked to my glasses, thick and black-rimmed, and stared.

I had thought that my soul died in Chicago, before Crystal was even conceived, but when she looked up at me with those cool brown-indigo eyes that wobbled and then focused on my face, my spirit stirred in the blackness of its dark sleep, and woke.

"Hello, baby," I said.

It was clear to me that she was her own person from the very start of things. And she didn't look like Michael, or Zho, or even Margie. "Is she smiling?" I asked as I fell in love.

"Maybe you better unwrap her, Margie, see if she filled her diaper," advised Grace. "Or maybe a pin's poking her."

~ ~ ~

I sometimes pretended that Crystal was mine, when she was a little girl in the Head Start room or when she slept at my house while Margie worked, after Zho Wash lost his strength and his sharpness. One of my sweetest memories is the time I handed her a Ritz cracker and she said in her darling little voice, so deep and scratchy, "Thank you, Mama." I didn't correct her but answered, "Oh, that's all right, Crystal; you are welcome."

I bought for Crystal things that I would have bought for my own girl: a Hello Kitty comb and brush set, pink corduroy overalls, a blue velvet winter coat with white furry trim. I made her a ribbon dress of lavender flowered calico, with a matching shawl and hair ties beaded with pansies; Margie and I tried not to show that we knew she was the prettiest little dancer at the powwow.

Sometimes I even imagined that Crystal looked like me, maybe just the smallest bit, though she didn't really; she looked, as she grew older, more like one of the LaForces. I look something like my own mother, Grace, but more like my dad, Roy Dionne, and thank goodness I inherited my dad's hair. Alice LaForce, the kindest lady on the reservation, told me once that I had been such a beautiful baby; however, by the time I reached my teens I could see that the incongruencies of my square jaw and long nose in combination with my wide cheekbones looked just plainly odd behind my Coke-bottle glasses. At the end of seventh grade I was as tall as I would ever be, which is not tall at all, and into young womanhood my middle never did thin out into any semblance of a waistline. I was, when I moved to Chicago the September after high school, built like a broad-shouldered ironing board.

Chicago. Sometimes I forget about Chicago for a little while.

Except for Grace and Roy, and the priest of course, I am the most devout Catholic in St. Francis parish. I am at church more than a lot of people because since Roy became all crippled up from his work he doesn't drive, and Grace, who never did learn to drive, can't walk distances anymore because of her ankles. So on Mass mornings I drive them to the church, leaving the house by six-thirty on Tuesdays and Thursdays and by eight-thirty on Sundays. Tuesdays after Mass my father and I listen to the radio in the car while Grace cleans the sacristy and the priest's room. Some Saturday afternoons I drive them to Confession, although I myself haven't gone to Confession since before I left for Chicago.

That's not exactly how it is. I go to confession in the sense that I drive to St. Francis, walk into the church, kneel next to Grace and Roy, and then stand behind them in line at the back of the church. When it is my turn I go into the confessional and kneel before the gauze-covered wooden lattice. When the priest slides open the window I am already silently praying my litany of sins but aloud I say, "Bless me, Father, for I have . . ." and list the venial pettinesses of the life I have come to lead.

How does one begin to ask forgiveness for sins rooted in unforgivable stupidity, in unforgivable weakness, when the Church says nothing about absolution for stupidity and weakness but only the simplicities of the sacrament? The Dale Ann who took the Greyhound to Chicago was too ignorant to sin; the Dale Ann who came back to Mozhay already fallen from grace by way of a weakness conceived in stupidity and birthed in willful iniquity.

The priest whispers his prayers of absolution on behalf of God and ends by telling me to go and sin no more. I answer, "Thank you, Father," stand and turn the small metal latch that is like an old ice box handle, and quietly walk over to the last row of pews to kneel next to my parents, saying my penance and becoming absolved, they assume.

In all these years since I came home from Chicago, and it's been three decades, St. Francis has gone through half a dozen priests: not one has refused me communion or while placing the Host in my cupped hands even looked closely to see if I might perhaps be the woman in the confessional, the woman who is not really absolved.

The Church calls it "Reconciliation" now, as though that makes any difference.

~ ~ ~

On the Greyhound ride from Chicago, snowy cold air blew across my face at the Duluth terminal when the driver opened the door. Awakened, I sat up. Outside the bus, the soldier with the sun-burned eyes was walking away, one arm holding the duffle on his shoulder and the other arm around a girl in a ski jacket.

I opened *Franny and Zooey* and reread half of it between Duluth and Tuomela's. As the Greyhound slowed at the Dionne Fork and the driver tapped the horn for anyone who was waiting inside the Skelly station for a ride to Canada, lovely Franny, who had, like me, fled from college, had arrived at home, her family's large New York apartment, where her mother had nestled her into a couch made up with pretty sheets and a fuzzy blanket.

That is where I stopped, that last time I read *Franny and Zooey*.

Jack's letter might still, today, hold my place on page 123 in Buff's discarded copy, which I never reopened and which has been lost somewhere in the years since that evening.

Just as I remembered and expected, at the sound of the horn my mother stopped whatever she was doing to peer from across the road, leaning slightly forward to see what was going on. I still hadn't thought of what to say to her, but because the passenger door opened away from her line of vision I hurried off the bus before it pulled away, holding onto my suitcase as tight as Sharon holding onto her baby, as the soldier his duffle, feeling my heart trip and flutter against its hard vinyl shell. With rounded shoulders I cowered and stumbled up swaying steps that needed paint, ducked to pull the door handle into the store at the same time that Mrs. Tuomela opened the door by bumping it out with her backside. I held the door open as she turned, holding both hands up as if she had just scrubbed for surgery.

"Nobody for the bus! Can't come out; I'm full of meat!" she called; upon seeing me, she lowered the pitch of her abrasive smoker's voice almost to a whisper, as though she thought that my mother could hear. "Well, Dale Ann! Pull the curtains, will you, so people will know we're closed. Got a minute to help me? Can you put the other bowl on the chair, wrap some pounds? Here, put down your bag, take off your coat." She stepped back of the counter and waved me in to join her.

Mrs. Tuomela was grinding meat for hamburger. Her left hand fed pieces of round, chuck, and fat into a heavy metal meat grinder clamped to the counter; as she turned the handle with her right hand, her shoulders and head swayed and swung. Half-moons of powder-scented sweat darkened the underarms of her cotton housedress and the front of her dress underneath her dropped, rhythmically swinging breasts; under the fluorescent light above the counter, sweat beads gleamed along her hairline and between her tight, quarter-sized pin curls.

I had helped dozens of times and knew she needed the bowl of hamburger lifted from the seat of the wooden chair under the meat grinder's spout and another bowl slid into its place quickly, before any hamburger hit the chair, and then doubled handfuls of hamburger to be wrapped in plastic and stacked in the freezer. The Tuomelas did this weekly, with a fresh slab of chuck as well as any meat that hadn't sold and was likely to spoil.

"Mr. Tuomela's in the cellar stoking the furnace, honey . . . Jorma! . . . JORMA! . . . Dale Ann's here!"

I heard his high voice and his slow dragging crawl up the narrow wooden stairs before I saw him. "Well, did she come back to work? We can sure use her," he nearly sang. Smiling, he lifted a crutch from its hook at the top of the stairs and step-hopped into the store. His matching Dickey's work shirt and pants were streaked with coal dust; one pants leg was neatly pinned to above the knee and one shirtsleeve to the opposite shoulder. "Are we glad to see you, girlie! Aren't we, Mother?"

No questions about Chicago. Just like that, I was back at the store, where I hid out in the apartment back of the counter, in the Tuomela living room, for the next twenty-four hours. By then I had taken a bath, put on clean clothes, and was as ready as I would ever be to cross the road and face my mother.

Grace was older than most mothers because she had married late. We never knew exactly how old she was, just that she looked more like a grandmother than a mother, and because she wasn't from Mozhay but from somewhere in Louisiana, it was impossible for Mrs. Minogeezhik and Beryl Duhlebon, the reservation experts on linkages between genealogy and behavioral and physical characteristics, to establish an explanation for her aggressive housekeeping and strict child rearing. Ambitious and thrifty, a scrubber and ironer, she never left the house with her hair in pin curls, and she always removed her apron before answering the door that in her peculiar and foreign way she kept latched, which prevented visitors from practicing the time-honored Mozhay custom of walking right in. She traveled a path paved with rumors as many and varied as little stones that she stepped on and over but never around, and without looking; in her wake they scattered, broke, rearranged themselves. She had had a family in the South that she abandoned when she met my father, was one; another was that she had been a hootchie-kootchie dancer when Roy met her in a bar. Mrs. Minogeezhik told Beryl that a friend of hers in Leech Lake knew for a fact that my mother was a Negro who was passing; Beryl told Mrs. Minogeezhik that was really Grace's own business but that she'd heard Grace had been a Holy Roller when she lived in the South but converted when she married my father. That might have explained why she never missed Mass and her enthusiasm for scouring the priest's bathtub and laundry every week. I never knew if any of these stories were true, only that Roy married Grace after he got out of the Army and that he brought her back up to Mozhay. My father was a lumberjack; before the work crippled him, he lived out in the woods half of every year. Us children, four girls and then our little brother, were born in late winter or early spring, near the end of five logging seasons in a row.

The next morning Mr. Tuomela and I played cards at the counter while we watched out the gas station window for the bus. It stopped right on time. No one got off at the station; the driver left a small stack of Duluth newspapers, and then the bus circled the Y and headed north for Canada. My mother would think that I had just been dropped off at Tuomela's. Wishing I was still a passenger, I picked up my suitcase and walked out of the store. Across the road the curtains moved; my mother stood at the window with her arms crossed, squinting, a dust rag in one hand.

My father once asked her, "How come you are so hard on these girls, anyway?"

"Because a woman's got a hard life ahead of her," she answered grimly. "A woman's got to be up to the job."

Until that moment when she saw me crossing the road, back

from the glory of my relocation job in Chicago, I had been a big part of Grace's plans for her life's future ease. She had pictured me earning a paycheck, sending money home, meeting some white man with a nice job, sending money home, inspiring my younger sisters to do the same, all of us sending money home, Grace sitting back and finally enjoying herself. Winters while my dad was away lumberjacking, she could just wait for all those checks coming in the mail and then call her friends to brag about her smart and successful daughters who would have liked to stay in Mozhay but were in such demand elsewhere. She would buy a nice front room set, a matching couch and chair with a coffee table and end tables and a pair of lamps, too, and save for when Roy retired; then they would buy a little camper and do some traveling.

Then she saw me, the first step on the road to her dreams, walking across the road from the Skelly station.

Her mouth opened, moved, moved again, rapidly. I walked through the yard and up the stairs, and opened the front door.

She was standing on the other side. "What in the name of aitch is going on?" she asked.

~ ~ ~

The next month was a difficult one.

Because my side of the bed had been given to Cecile when I left, I slept rolled in a blanket on the floor directly below her trailing hand and arm that, because she was a restless sleeper, tapped in patterns on the mattress and bed rail, brushed my nose, flailed and waved, and once bounced a fist against the side of my head as she muttered, "Open the door, Annette! Open it!"

My mother avoided looking at me; when she did, she glared. When she spoke, it was to tell me only what she thought necessary: that she was going into town with Yvonne, that I would need to get supper ready, that the floors were dirty and needed washing, that when my dad came out of the woods after lumberjack season I would have to tell him about this myself.

"I don't know what this will do to him," she said ominously.

So there I was, no longer a shining example to my sisters and my little brother and all the other kids at school, and a letdown for the entire reservation. A disappointment to my high school teachers, to the relocation worker who was expected to visit the house after school sometime next month to talk with Grace about Yvonne.

But I had a job. Every morning except for Sundays I arrived at the store early to open with Mr. Tuomela, who unlocked the front door and turned on the gas pump lights, then hung up his crutch and slid and bumped down the stairs to shovel more coal into the furnace. Back in the apartment Mrs. Tuomela stepped heavily back and forth, back and forth, thumping and creaking the floorboards as she washed up, dressed, and put on the coffee. As the stovetop percolator belched, at first lightly and sporadically, then more rapidly and deeply, she opened the front curtains and then cooked breakfast: eggs and oatmeal, or eggs and pancakes. After a month or so, most mornings when the eggs were just beginning to congeal I would know it by the smell and would run into the little toilet stall, the one they put in at the front of the store for customers, to throw up.

There was no way or setting that could have made telling Grace that I was pregnant any easier than just doing it. I did practice. Alone in the store, while the Tuomelas were in Mesabi at the clinic, I said it while wiping off the tops of a case of canned peas with a damp rag: "I'm pregnant." Grace never used that word; she seemed to think it was vulgar. She always said "expecting" in one of two ways: in a normal voice she sounded as if she meant expecting something you wanted or had a right to want; in a whisper she meant shame and disgrace. So I couldn't say to Grace that

I was pregnant, and what if I said I was expecting, and she said expecting what, and then I had to explain? That would be worse. "I'm going to have a baby." That would bring it home but make it much too real for me.

The way she finally found out, I took the car to Mesabi to go to the Pamida and also SuperValu, where we got most of our groceries because Tuomela's only sold canned goods and meat, and I forgot to buy a box of sanitary napkins to replace the one that was almost empty. We all, my sisters and I, took them as we needed out of the big box in the bedroom closet. Well, I forgot. I got all the way home and Grace said, "You forgot the list"; I said, "I saw it before I left so I think I got everything"; Yvonne said, "Where's the box of Modess?" I said, "Oh shoot, I forgot"; and Yvonne said, "Corn sakes, Dale Ann, how could you forget something like that?" and just like that Grace gave me a sharp look that I pretended not to see. And there was no escaping her; she waited patient and unblinking, watchful as a cat. When she saw me go out the back door for the outhouse she followed me into the yard and grabbed my arm. She hissed, "Are you *pregnant*?" When I couldn't find the words to answer, she staggered and grabbed my arm with her other hand too. I supported my mother in this way as we walked to the rectory, where she told me to sit on the porch while she talked with the priest.

As I waited I told myself that I had known all along that I couldn't just go on helping out Mr. and Mrs. Tuomela for fifty cents an hour, pumping gas and cleaning and grinding meat while I grew bigger and bigger, giving birth, stashing the baby in the apartment with Mrs. Tuomela whenever I went home, Grace never suspecting a thing.

It was all planned and decided by Grace and the priest. She told me that it would kill my dad if he knew, and so nobody would tell him. Or my sisters. Or anybody at all. I would go to Duluth, to a home for unwed mothers, where I would work for my keep.

Grace would tell people that I had decided to become a nun and was living in a convent.

The morning I left she cut my hair short, the way the nuns wore theirs under their veils, she said, and gave me a scarf to wear on the bus trip, to cover my choppy hair and my shame. My thick head of hair had always provided me some cover and, truth be told, a little bit of prettiness, too, I'd thought. Without it, I was exposed to everything in the world I was afraid of; I tried not to let it show but failed, of course. Roy came back from lumber camp especially to see me off to the convent. He stood all teary-eyed next to Grace, once again so proud of his little girl Dale Ann, who had graduated from high school, and worked in Chicago, and was going to the convent to become a nun. Grace looked proud, too, of the Dale Ann she had herself re-created and appeared to almost believe in: pious, shorn Dale Ann who would be letting them know shortly what saint's name she had picked to be known by.

I failed, too, at looking like I felt chosen and inspired by the Holy Spirit, when what I felt was completely defeated. And I had lost what was my only good physical feature, that heavy veil of hair that was to be in my mother's fabrication of pride and untruth replaced by a wimple.

~ ~ ~

I spent the next four months on the home's schedule, rising early in the morning, doing my rotation of cooking and cleaning duties, tutoring other girls with their high school work, studying for catechism class, and singing with the Little Flowers, the pregnant girls' choir. Afternoons we worked in the basement sorting through donated merchandise for the St. Vincent de Paul store. Evenings we had prayers, leisure reading, and letter writing. I never wrote to anybody. Grace had told everyone in Mozhay that the convent rules wouldn't allow letters until I took my final vows.

My getting money from the county to pay for the hospital

hinged on my telling them who had gotten me in trouble. In saying his name aloud the memory surfaced and reared like a silent banshee: sweating red face, salty and urine-scented fingers, a fist pressed against my cheekbone, the pain, the bleeding that for some reason I had been certain meant that I couldn't be pregnant—all of that seemed to fill my lungs, body, and existence in that one breath. I was asked, I inhaled, I spoke his name, his heavy fingers clenched and squeezed that part of my body that was no longer my own. And, with that, my body and my future became the county's property.

Dear Jack,

My but you are probably surprised to hear from me. I hope that you are fine and taking care of yourself. Your Mother says you are a Sergeant now. She is very proud of you.

I am writing about Dale Ann, she is back from Chicago but in Duluth now. She is in the Convent and going to be a Sister. She is a Novice. Can't write because the rules say no letters with Novices. So I am writing. She can't get letters either. So don't write to her, she won't get it.

She's doing good at the Convent and before too long she will be a Bride of Christ. The way she likes to read, she might maybe even be a Teacher when she's done.

Sincerely yours,

Mrs. Grace Dionne

In the hospital I shared a labor room with a married girl, a white girl whose husband was there at the side of her bed on a little wheeled stool the entire time except for when the nurses kicked him out for our preps and the examinations to measure the dilation of our cervixes. She was a pretty thing, all made up and shampooed for the occasion. She arrived during my fifth hour of pacing the floor and timing labor pains, and I was glad to have the company. The first thing the labor room nurse made her do was wash her face and take off her false eyelashes; then the nurse asked me to braid her hair. After her prep, she put on a pink quilted bathrobe trimmed with eyelet lace and pink fuzzy slippers, and sat cross-legged on her bed to wait for her husband. Even in all that pink fluffiness, with her hair pulled back and her ears sticking out in translucent scallops, she looked like a little boy and scared to death. The sight of me, heavy and short of breath, my face swollen with the pressure of labor pains, didn't help.

After a while she began to squeal at the start of each labor pain, then to weep, to scream, then after the pain subsided to apologize to her husband for screaming. "I'm sorry, honey," she said, her pale lips and wide eyes inches from his waxen, sick expression. "It just hurts so bad," and then it would start again, with the sweet, freckled little thing swearing worse than those college girls in Chicago. This repeated itself every ten minutes, then every five, for another hour; at that point the nurse told her she was ready to deliver and they all left, unnerved husband to a waiting room and the nurse and girl to the delivery room. Through the pillows I held to each side of my head as, over my loud humming of "Salve Regina," the only song I could recall, I listened to her shriek and cuss in some room far down the hall for another twenty minutes. In the silence that must have indicated her elevation to motherhood, I realized I had begun to hold my breath and count the seconds of my own cresting and crashing contractions.

"Well, heavenly days, what a nice fast delivery that was!" the nurse exclaimed cheerily when she returned to the labor room. "Oh. My." She stared; I realized she was looking at my legs, which were writhing in complete disconnect from the stillness of the rest of my body. A samurai sword with a dulled and rusted blade, driven deep in the small of my back, was forcing, forcing its way toward my belly, and my baby, which it would slice in half. I groaned, groaned.

The nurse sat on the bed. Her heavy, hard hip pressed against mine; she leaned toward me and said that it was time to breathe slo-o-o-wly, slo-o-owly. I turned my face to the wall; she reached for my chin and turned it back. "Breeeeeeathe, breeeeathe, slo-o-o-o-owly, slo-o-o-o-owly." Again I turned to the wall; I groaned, more loudly. This time she took my face in both hands and brought her own face close to mine. Her eyes, gray-green stones, looked deep into mine, and I saw she knew that I was inhuman, after all, only the incubator for a baby that would belong to someone else; that I had no husband to sit with me in the labor room, that there would be no witnesses to anything she might say. "Stop it," she hissed. "Stop it, Dale Ann; you know and I know it can't possibly hurt that much."

It was not my intent to knock her off the bed and onto the floor, but that is what happened next. A tall woman and brawnier than me, with arms like Mrs. Tuomela's, she rolled right up off the hard and dusty tiles as if she had done that before, and I sensed her pulling her right arm back ready to hit me so I too rolled, rolled right off the bed and onto my feet ready to face her, and as we squared off the samurai sword reached my belly, breaking the amniotic sac with a pop. And what seemed like gallons and gallons of shockingly hot water gushed, and gushed again, onto my feet and the floor. I raised my head and my arms and my voice to God, who might have been one of the ceiling tiles but probably wasn't, and begged, "Help me! Somebody help me! I don't want to have a baby!"

My impression of the delivery room was brief, a brilliant whiteness lit up like the inside of a lightbulb but cold as ice. I lay on a narrow plastic table and was directed to lift my feet and legs onto gleaming chrome stirrups. "They hurt; they're too high," I whined, dignity lost, while the nurse, ignoring me, tethered my wrists to cleats at the side of the table. "Does the light bother you? Do you want to see the baby when it is born?" she asked, and I shook my head. She tied a blindfold over my eyes and the whiteness vanished, though not the cold. "I hope that it dies," my voice throbbed into the darkness, and then I shuddered uncontrollably, keening without sound.

"I think we'll need to give this one the orange gas." The voice of an amused male. "Here we go, Dale Ann." A rubber-smelling mask was held heavily over my nose and mouth; I gagged on air heavy with cloves. "Count to ten, Dale Ann; come on . . . one . . . two-o-o . . . thre-e-e-e . . . fo-o-o-o-our . . ."

"What a relief," someone said from far away; then, urgently and close, "the cord! Here we go!" and a century later, ". . . she's a tubal, isn't she?"

~ ~ ~

I woke in pain to the white room again, empty except for another nurse, this one a girl my age. "Good morning, Dale Ann," she said. I moved my arms that were no longer tied down, crooked one behind my head, and retched. Warm vomit ran down the side of my mouth, down my neck to my armpit and breast; in seconds it was cold. "Aw," she said, patting my shoulder. She ran water into a basin and gently washed me. "Is that better? Are you warm enough? Does your belly hurt?" My belly, covered by white blankets, rose to a mound higher than my breasts; pain radiated stiffly past the linty diamond-patterned weave, blurring my vision.

"Did I have a baby?"

"A healthy bouncing baby . . . (she stopped before saying if it was a boy or a girl); you've made a mother very happy."

To the side of my head was a rattle like spoons and forks in the silverware drawer; groaning, I turned to see what it was.

"You've had a caesarean delivery, Dale Ann." An older nurse was lining instruments up on trays, neat as a place setting in home ec class, that she placed in a stainless steel cupboard. The instruments looked strange and menacing, shaped for bizarre and specific purposes that I tried not to imagine. The room began to spin slowly, and then I took the slow deep breaths that I hadn't in the labor room.

"Can you get me out of here?" My tongue was the size of a cow's, thick in my mouth. Could she understand me?

"In a minute; Miss Nelson will bring you to your room. First, though, Doctor needs you to sign something."

"What is it?"

"Doctor's orders."

In signing I gave my permission for the Indian Health Service to pay for the fallopian tubal ligation that had been done while I was still under anesthetic, which saved the county money, time, and the unpleasantness of dealing with a conscious young woman who might have regretted wishing that the baby that belonged to some happy mother was dead. Or, God forbid, have ever decided that she might wish to have another baby, a child of her own.

Sometimes I wish that I had seen my baby, no, the baby who was never mine, just once. Later on I found out that some girls were allowed to do that, but I didn't know to ask. I overheard one of the nurses telling another that there was a woman waiting for my baby on the condition that it looked white. If I had made her so happy, it must have looked white.

Perhaps her golden hair, as curly as Grace's, stood out from her head in a halo, and the small stars in her eyes lit up like Jack's when she smiled. I might have named her Jennifer.

~ ~ ~

The county had arranged for me to stay in the hospital for a week, then at the YWCA until I found a job. On my last day in the hospital I had two visitors. The first, a social worker, said that she would pick me up the next day and bring me to the Y and that she would try to get me an interview with Northwestern Bell. The second was Beryl, who had come to pick me up and take me back to Mozhay.

Beryl told me that earlier in the day when she had heard from Mrs. Tuomela that I was in the hospital in Duluth with an appendicitis attack, she got a ride home as fast as she could and cut right through the woods over to the allotment house where thank goodness Zho Washington was home, giving a bath to one of his dogs that had gotten into a fight with a skunk. He'd rinsed the poor thing off quick and locked it into the lean-to with some clean water, and he and Beryl hit the road, making it to Duluth before I got released. Right in front of the social worker Beryl told me to not sign any adoption papers until a copy of the baby's birth certificate was sent to the Ar-Bee-See's enrollment office, and she sat there with me until the worker got us a copy. Beryl put it into her purse for safekeeping. Then I signed the adoption papers, the worker and Beryl witnessed, we packed my things into my suitcase, and I was free to leave. A nurse came into the room with a wheelchair; she placed the suitcase across my lap where I would have held a baby if I had been bringing one home, and wheeled me down the hall, out the door, and to the pick-up curb, where Zho Wash was waiting in his truck.

That Zho, he is so quiet that he just nodded and settled me in the middle of the front seat without saying a word. Halfway to Sweetgrass he took a twist of strawberry licorice out of his shirt pocket and offered it to me. Miserable though I was, holding that fragrant candy in my hand as it grew warm and sticky, when Beryl tore it into three pieces and she and Zho Wash began to chew, I did the same.

~ ~ ~

Back at home, some things had changed. For one thing, I once again had a bed. Yvonne had gotten married and moved to Mesabi. Her husband got hired on at the mines, and she clerked at the Ben Franklin. They were saving for a down payment on a house. Annette had quit school and was engaged to one of the Dommages who was at the Marine boot camp in San Diego; they planned to marry before he went overseas. She spent much of her time reading bridal magazines and driving Grace and Cecile around to rummage sales and the Salvation Army store in Mesabi.

Grace told everyone that I had decided not to become a nun, after all, but that the vow of chastity I had taken in the convent couldn't be revoked and so I wouldn't ever be getting married. Also, that she thought the shorter hair was an improvement.

I felt invisible around the house, not unwelcome so much as unnoticed. Grace's life had become closer to the life she had always wanted. Now that she had something to hold her head up over and talk about besides her story about me in the convent, she emerged from her cocoon of worry about her girls to become, for Grace, almost a social butterfly. She also became a regular drop-in visitor at Tuomelas' (although she always brought her own cup of coffee, in order to not waste the dime) and at the RBC (no need to bring her own coffee, as it was free for the Elders), where she could brag modestly about her daughters' lives, luck, and accomplishments.

When Mozhay received federal money for its own Head Start program, I applied for a job and was hired by the RBC. I have worked with little kids ever since. It keeps me busy, and I love the work. Yet, although ever since I got back home I have always had a lot going on, taking care of my mother and dad, and helping Margie out with Crystal during all of Zho Washington's troubles with his wife and his health, and all those little Head Start dumplings, sometimes, when I am by myself in the teacher's lounge or while watching TV after Grace and Roy go to bed, I feel lonely.

After Jack got home from the service, he telephoned the house every once in a while, asking for me. Grace told him I wasn't home. At the gas station, at Pamida, at Mass, at the spring and fall powwows, I avoided him. All things considered, that was a blessing. I was grateful for Grace's way of thinking, which protected me from what was really unbearable. And there was Crystal, of course, who I could pretend was my own at Head Start and when I watched her while Margie worked, and then the worrying I did along with Margie when Crystal got a little older took up so much of all our time that one evening when I sat down for the Rosary with Grace and Roy, I realized that I hadn't thought about Chicago all day.

However, I never stopped thinking about Jack, and I watched as his life progressed, parallel to mine and separate.

While he was in the service and perhaps waiting for the letter that I began and never finished, Jack had most of his pay sent home every month to his mother. Mrs. Minogeezhik was a widow who adored her boy and had big plans for him: She spent just about nothing from his checks but deposited most of the money in a joint savings account, taking pleasure and satisfaction in the reading of her and her boy's monthly bank statements. By the time Jack's enlistment was over, she had learned all about compound interest and could hardly contain herself while she waited at the Skelly station for his bus. She had the most recent bank statement in her purse, and within five minutes after leaping from the stairs right into his arms she had him sitting at the little table Mrs. Tuomela had set up inside the front door for "Fresh Coffee N Hot Lunch," her latest moneymaking venture, reading figures from forty-eight months of army paydays.

Mrs. Minogeezhik advised Jack to stay living at her house and invest his money in a business, so Jack leased the outbuilding next to the Skelly station and opened a garage and bodyshop, with his mother as office manager and bookkeeper. When the Tuomelas retired a few years later, they sold the gas station, store, and forty acres of land back of it to Jack, who took out a mortgage large enough to add an apartment above the store for his mother. The partners worked and prospered. My cousin Eugene was hired to run the garage, and after Zho's first heart attack Jack hired Margie to manage the store, which had been renamed "Minogeezhik Adaawaagamig." Jack and his mother next bought a small construction and painting company in Mesabi. In 1982 the Mozhay Point RBC offered to buy five acres of Minogeezhik property in back of the store for a combined school and bingo hall. Jack sold; Minogeezhik Builders and Painters bid the job and contracted the entire operation; a decade later, after the bingo parlor paid off the school building, the RBC bought twenty more acres from Jack and built the Chi Waabik Casino in the Woods. Minogeezhik Enterprises built the new casino and retained the entertainment and food service rights; between the reservation and the Minogeezhik family, enough jobs were added to Mozhay Point that unemployment all but disappeared.

Jack and his mother had become the most prosperous people on the entire reservation. They established John Minogeezhik Friends, a nonprofit foundation named in honor of Jack's late father, which provided a variety of grants and low-interest loans for band members and programs, and Jack and his mother became the most respected and, truth be told, powerful people on the entire reservation.

Eventually Jack ran for and won the office of Tribal Chair of Mozhay Point. At his swearing-in his mother stood by his side, and the Head Start children and I, in our new special-occasion ribbon shirts and moccasins paid for by John Minogeezhik Friends, sat in the front row with the Head Start Foster Grandmothers, among them Beryl and her friend Sis. The room quieted as Jack raised his right hand and took a breath before swearing to serve the Mozhay Point Band of Ojibwe and uphold our tribal constitution. In that pause I heard Sis whisper to Beryl, "That boy could use a wife."

Nisswi: The Wild Ricers

Margie-enjiss

1973

AT THE MOZHAY POINT INDIAN RESERVATION's late summer powwow in 1973, not that long before he would become Margie's ricing partner and then flee to Minneapolis, Michael Washington danced in his father's moccasins. A folded blue bandanna wrapped across his forehead and tied in back held his hair in place and framed his face, which he had painted black with a narrow white stripe across the eyes. Michael's face looked fierce, predatory, superhuman; his feet appeared to not quite touch the dusty ground of the powwow circle. For the rest, he was dressed in his everyday street clothes: secondhand corduroy jeans, a graying white T-shirt with a frayed neck, and a plaid cowboy shirt, pearl-covered snaps left unfastened, that after the next wash would be missing its elbows. Although he was not the only dancer dressed in both powwow and street clothes, the combination of his outfit with the face paint and his nearly perfect dancing was eye-catching.

Spectators who watched from lawn chairs around the powwow circle turned their heads to watch Michael dance; dancers inside the circle followed the spectators' heads with their eyes; Michael didn't seem to notice. He danced as if he were alone in his mother's apartment in Minneapolis or in the woods outside his father's cabin at Sweetgrass, or in an empty powwow arena, his shoulders tracing figure eights through the air in the powwow circle, one rising as the other dipped, the breadth he carried above the ribs balanced recklessly over his much smaller hips and legs; below, his father's beaded and ribbon-trimmed moccasins purposefully yet lightly, almost playfully, double-stomped left-left-right-right on that eighth-inch of air between Michael and the ground.

"Who's *that*?" a young woman traditional dancer in beaded black velour asked her friend. From across the powwow circle they turned their heads to watch him dance, which caught the attention of the friend's brother, who was drumming and singing. With the hand not holding a drumstick he covered his heart; he batted his eyes at Michael, then at his sister, teasing her. Shooting him a dirty look she brushed her friend's elbow with hers, and the girls concentrated on their dancing, ignoring both men.

Michael passed Margie and Theresa, who toe-heeled so carefully in their chunky clogs that the hand-tied fringe on the shawls they wore over their stylish embroidered peasant blouses and jeans barely swayed. From the fierceness of his black and white face he glanced down, amused by their dainty steps and small female feet in bulky shoes; his bashfully brilliant smile ricocheted from his mouth to the floor to Margie's rib cage, where it bounced and danced, as she had known it would if she ever saw him again, in a beat somewhere between that of her heart and the drum.

"It's Michael!" Theresa exclaimed to Margie. "Did you see that was Michael, in the face paint?"

Margie nodded, then pointed her lips slightly in the direction of Michael's back. "There he goes." In order to stay behind him so that she could watch him dance, she shortened her step; Theresa understood and matched her step to Margie's.

As the girls behind him watched, Michael raised his tobacco pouch. His feet pivoted *shuffle ball change*, the double-stomp turned to a triple within a four-four beat, his shoulders and arms became wings, his chin jerked, and Michael shape-shifted into a raven. He danced in powerful near flight; his stomp became a rush of wings, and as he broke tether from the ground, a shifting pulse of electric azure blue from the sole of one beaded moccasin caught Margie's eye with every step change from left to right, lighting in his wake the path he broke for the dancers behind him. She tasted canned blueberries and in a split second relived the afternoon last winter at Zho Wash's house. She took a deep breath. *Jiibik*, she thought. Magic.

A fancy dancer in scarlet satin bounded like a pursued deer into the space between Margie and Michael; with her hands on her hips she bounced on the balls of her feet; her shawl spread and spun, blocking Michael from Margie's sight. When the dancer sprang back to the outside edge of the circle, Michael was gone, and Margie's eyes were empty.

That was at the late summer powwow, the season after they met and the year before Michael fled down I-35 right in the middle of ricing, gone overnight it seemed, like the Lost Lake geese who flew south in autumn. He flew only as far south as Minneapolis, like a lot of people did from reservations up north, Indians on the road with a destination in mind, looking for work, for opportunity, for relatives who were homesick. To escape for a while. When their hearts' seasons changed, they flew back home, in a migratory pattern that had come to seem as natural and inevitable as the patterns of birds.

~ ~ ~

Late summer into early fall is when wild rice, *manoomin*, ripens and is ready to harvest, its heads heavy and nodding on the green stalks that grow up out of Lost Lake, sometimes taller than a man's head. A year after the late summer powwow when his son had danced in his moccasins, Zho Wash decided he was too old to rice. "I'm not going out this year," he told Michael. "If you want rice you're gonna have to do it yourself, find yourself a ricing partner.

Go ask that Margie Robineau; her dad used to rice and she looks like a good worker. I'm too old for this stuff."

That was how Margie and Michael got to be ricing partners. Zho Wash drove them to the boat landing in his blue Chevy truck that sounded like a helicopter, helped them unload his rowboat and duckbill, knockers, gunnysacks, and the lunch he had packed in a grocery bag for Michael and Margie. He pulled a crushed-looking straw hat from under the seat, his ricing hat, and offered it to Margie ("It'll keep the sun out of your eyes, my girl"), who said, "Migwech, I'll take good care of it." At the landing Zho Wash made a tobacco offering and said a prayer, helped Michael push the rowboat out onto the lake. "See youse later," he said, as Michael jumped into the boat, and went to sit at the campfire, where some older ladies were making coffee.

They worked well together, Michael and Margie. He poled with the duckbill; she sat in the middle of the boat and knocked rice hulls onto the gunnysack spread in front of her. They didn't speak; Margie listened to Michael hum his ricing song, then songs from the radio, and worked the rhythm of knocking rice, left knock-knock, right knock-knock, to the rhythm of his soft voice. A beautiful day, she thought. He finished "Blackbird," paused between songs.

"Mino-giizhigad," she commented.

"Ay-yuh, onishishin," he answered. "It's a pretty day." He pulled the duckbill up from the mud on the bottom of the lake, pushed it back down; she heard the swish and ripple of the boat moving through the water, and talk and laughter from other people out on the lake. "Goodbye, Ruby Tuesday; who could hang a name on you?" he sang under his breath.

"A beautiful morning," Margie thought to herself. "I will remember this song, and the softness of the sunlight, and the breeze, light as sheer curtains blowing in an open window. I will remember this morning with Michael, that today is a warm day, that the sky is a purely, deeply blue dome over Lost Lake, that I can almost feel Michael, can imagine that I am Michael, back of me, pushing the boat forward over the water, through rice stalks as tall as he is. Now his shadow cools me, as the boat moves away from the sun. If I turn around I will see him; his hair, getting damp as he gets warm from the work, working its way loose from the bandanna tied around his head. I can see him without even looking. I will always remember this."

"Are your arms getting sore?" Michael asked, and she realized that she had been sitting motionless while he had been poling the boat through a particularly thick and loaded stand of wild rice stalks.

"Gaawiin, I'm fine; just leaving some for the ducks." She concentrated on ricing: left, knock-knock, right, knock-knock. She ignored bugs lighting on her arms, wiped sweat from her face with her sleeves without breaking the rhythm of working with Michael.

Eventually, the hard work of ricing intruded on her body and on her thoughts. Margie's arms and shoulders began to tire, then to ache, and she ignored the pain as long as she could stand to, not wanting the memory she was making to be interrupted. She flexed her arms down, her shoulders up, as unobtrusively as she could, continued to match her work rhythm, left, knock-knock, right, knock-knock, to Michael poling with the duckbill; then her arms began to shake with fatigue, and she began to count to herself, right, knock-knock, left, knock-knock, to keep the rhythm. "Are you going to Scarborough fair? Parsley, sage, rosemary, and thyme," she hummed as sweat stung her eyes, and couldn't remember how the rest of the song went.

"Getting tired yet?" Michael asked.

"Gawiin; well, no, just a little bit." She struggled, concentrated. "Remember me to one who lives there; she once was a true love of mine." Her knocking grew uneven, ragged; the boat had turned, and they were moving almost directly toward the sun;

light began to shoot jagged hot patterns in front of her left eye; she shook her head to clear it.

"Gi bakade, na? Want lunch?" he asked. "I'm getting pretty hungry; gotta stop for a while and eat."

Gratefully, she lay the knockers on the bottom of the boat and said, "Eya, wiisini daa."

They ate the pile of baloney and cheese sandwiches that Zho Wash had packed for them in a paper grocery bag and shared the plastic jug of grape Kool-Aid. Margie looked out over the rice stalks growing from the lake, letting the wind cool her face, and turned from Michael so that he wouldn't see how closely she watched him.

Michael lit a cigarette, asked Margie, "Hey, sagaswaa?"

"No. Thanks, though." Margie didn't smoke. She stuffed wadded-up waxed paper from the sandwiches into the grocery bag. In Michael's shadow she inhaled his smoke along with the air of the beautiful day, sweet with rice, growing and green, smoky from not only Michael's cigarette but also the burned cedar from the smudging he had done that morning. She breathed in and out, in and out, until the elusive mystery of the day, of rice growing and green, cigarette smoke and smudged cedar, settled in her lungs and then on her face, throat, chest, and arms, on the places where her friends the little bottle spirits, the conjoined twins optimism and confidence, usually lit when she drank, giving her company and courage.

"Got a puff?" she asked.

"You sure?" He sounded surprised. "You're not a smoker, are you?"

"Sometimes."

"You really want one? Naw, you're not old enough to smoke yet."

His teasing was sunlight showering weightless flecks of yellow happiness in random, repeating patterns as seductive as the dance of the bottle spirits on her arms, her face, her hair. She raised her face to speak directly, closely into his. "Sagaswaa, daga."

Margie took the cigarette from his offering hand, brushing his fingers with her own, and held it as Michael did, between her second and third fingers, filter end just inside her hand. She raised her hand to cover her mouth as she inhaled, cupped as Michael did, faking a drag in order not to cough; she hated smoking. She handed the cigarette back to Michael, this time brushing her fingers accidentally, lightly, against the tender inside of his wrist. Leaning toward him she knelt, fit her shoulders inside the half circle of his, and raised her face to look again directly, closely, into his. Curving one hand over the solid muscle between his shoulder and neck, she caressed and smoothed his lips with the other, cupped it under his jaw, brought her own face to his, closed her eyes. Her kiss was light; breathing with Michael she felt as though the skin on their noses and cheeks had melted and merged into an intimate, cedar-scented sweetness.

Then Michael leaned backward, away from Margie, who opened her eyes. "I love you," she told him.

And Michael didn't answer. He looked up at the sky; his jaw shaded her eyes; she watched his pulse beat once, twice, on his neck. Once, twice again. And again.

Above, a drifting cloud uncurled to a rabbit dying in a snare that tightened as it kicked, the winter whiteness of its fur blending into the surrounding snow; a young man's bent elbows moved quickly once, twice.

Michael's silence was pitying and sorrowful, louder than a shout of disgust, or ridicule, or laughter, longer than the years it must have taken for Zho Wash to carve and polish the rice knockers and wear them with his hands to the smoothness Margie felt when, to cover the glare and void of her exposure, she picked them up from the bottom of the boat and asked, "Think we've got enough rice? Or do you want to rice some more?" Her voice, usually breathy and low, sounded to her high-pitched and tight, as though she were swallowing as she spoke.

"Let's go get this weighed," he answered, "see what we've got."

On the way back to the boat landing, she kept Zho Wash's hat pulled closely around the sides of her face and the back of her neck.

At the landing he told her to stay in the rowboat and stepped carefully out into knee-deep water to pull Margie and the rice to dry land. Zho Wash, Michael, and Margie bagged the damp, green rice in burlap sacks; Michael and Zho hung the sacks of the rice that they would sell over the hook on the rice buyer's scale, then loaded them onto his truck bed for the trip to his processing plant north of the Tweten road. Michael and Margie split the cash, twenty dollars each at fifty cents a pound for the eighty pounds they sold. Zho Wash and Michael loaded the rest, fifty pounds or so, into the trunk of the car.

Zho and Michael dropped Margie at the end of her Aunt Beryl's driveway. As they drove away Zho commented, "She's pretty quiet, Margie."

"Tired," Michael answered. "She isn't used to ricing."

~ ~ ~

Not long afterward, Margie didn't know when, Michael left Sweetgrass. It was Beryl who told her that Zho Wash seemed to be living alone again. "Big help he was with wild ricing, that Michael; left his dad with all that green rice to finish all by himself before it could go bad," the older woman commented. "Can't count on him for anything; you're better off staying away from him. Lots of nice young men around Sweetgrass; have you ever met Fred Simon, the one Mrs. Minogeezhik calls her honorary son? Now, there's a nice young man who works hard: he's been a big help to Mrs. Minogeezhik while her boy's in the Army, never gets into any trouble."

Margie didn't reply that without Michael there was no reason for her to remain at Sweetgrass. Instead she answered that she had stayed at Beryl's too long and should probably be getting back to Duluth and her job. Then Margie packed her clothes and began to walk toward the Dionne Fork, telling herself that maybe Jupiter would need her back.

When she had gone perhaps a mile she was picked up by the rice buyer, who said he could take her as far as the gas station at the Dionne Fork. At the gas station she used the bathroom and bought a pack of gum from Dale Ann, who Beryl's ladyfriend Sis had said was the nicest of the Dionne sisters ("the only nice one," were her exact words). Then Margie began the walk back toward Sweetgrass and was picked up by one of the Dommage brothers, who dropped her at the end of Beryl's driveway. From there she cut through the woods to Zho Wash's cabin, which is where he found her the next morning, awake and exhausted, on the front porch.

She had listened to the sounds of the old man waking at dawn: he had coughed, stretched and groaned, walked out the back door, stood silently. She heard him mumble his morning prayer, in Ojibwe, listened as he walked out into the woods to urinate, heard his footsteps splash through a puddle next to the back door when he returned to the house and opened the back door, listened as he lit the woodstove and ran water. He rattled pots and pans on the stove burner; when he stirred them, the scraping sound of metal spoon on metal pot made her teeth ache.

Inside, the old man set a bowl of venison and oatmeal soup on the table. From another saucepan he poured day-old coffee into a mug and stood for moment sipping and thinking; through the front window he saw the bowed back of a young woman sitting on the stoop.

Margie turned to the sound of the front door opening and to the scorched smell of reheated coffee.

"Nice morning," said Zho Wash. "Mino giizhigad noongoom, ina? Would you like some coffee?"

"Do you know where Michael is?" Margie asked.

"Oh, I think it's Mishiimini-Odanaa, where he was going."

"Where is that?"

"Mishimini-Odanaa, Apple Town; you know, Minneapolis? That's like a little joke, Mishimini-Odana. Apple-town, Minnie-apple-iss."

Margie tried to smile, and to laugh politely.

"Biindigen, Margie; come inside. Come in and have something to eat. Want some oatmeal soup?"

"I guess I'm not very hungry. It smells good, though." Tears ran down her cheeks to her jaw, dropped onto her sweatshirt. "Well, maybe."

Zho Wash thinned the denseness of the coffee with a little water and set it back over the fire to heat. Because Margie was company, he opened a can of evaporated milk and poured a generous amount into each of their cups, stirring in several sugars. The cup he handed to Margie had grounds swirling in circles on the surface. She cried silently, watching their patterns.

"Have some soup, my girl. It's good for you; you'll feel better." He filled Lucy's favorite bowl from the pot. "Here, you eat. I'll just be outside. I'm going to be parching rice today, have to get that done." He left the girl at the table.

The soup was good, although a little thin. Zho Wash had boiled water and thrown in a handful of oatmeal and another of chopped dried venison, then peppered it generously. Crying, she ate the bowlful and crying, stood at the window to watch the old man.

In the front yard Zho Wash built a fire inside a circle of stones. From the shed behind the house he dragged an old iron kettle, which he set on top of four large stones within the circle; then from the lean-to by the back door he carried a gunnysack of green rice and a wooden paddle. He poured rice into the kettle and stirred; when steam stopped rising from the kettle, he tipped the parched rice onto a canvas tarp and began another batch. Margie had not seen wild rice being parched by hand before, and still crying, she watched Zho Wash repeat the task, and repeat it again and again, always with an unhurried rhythm that oddly soothed her and finally mesmerized her. She felt sleepy and decided to lie on the couch for a few minutes to rest her eyes, which felt dry and salty while at the same time continued to drip tears and tears. She slept until the next day.

When she woke, Zho Wash was not in the cabin. On the table he had left a note, "Gone to town, back pretty soon." Reading it, she blinked and squinted and realized that the discomfort was caused by her being temporarily out of tears. Cried out for the time being, she drank several cups of coffee and saw, through her red and scratchy eyes, that the corners of the cabin floor were grimy, the windows gray with dust and dried rain. She searched the cabin until she found a broom in the lean-to and began to sweep.

Margie told herself that she would stay just until things were cleaned up and straightened out, as a favor back to Zho Wash for the soup. After that was done she would leave, she told herself, taking comfort in the magnitude of the task. She found a bucket in the shed and a box of Ivory Snow. Back of the door to the bedroom was a bag of rags. "I can just stay in the house; I don't even have to go outside, except to clean up the yard," she thought. Replenished by the coffee, her eyes dripped a fresh supply of tears into the bucket of soapy water.

Margie became a ghost, spending the days haunting the cabin while Zho Wash worked. After he had finished the season's rice and brought some to town to sell it, he began the next season's task, cutting wood pulp, which he sold in town, too. While he worked, and while he was gone, Margie straightened up the kitchen, washed the windows, sanded down the tabletop until it was soft as peach skin. Hunted through the shed and under the front and back stairs for the old man's bottles, drank only what she needed from them, and re-hid them.

Zho Wash acted as if it were a natural thing, that silent young woman sleeping on his sofa, walking the floor of the cabin, leaving the imprint of her cleaning, weeping from time to time, drinking his liquor. He threw the bottles out into the woods when they were empty and found new hiding places for their replacements. Every day until late afternoon he let her work, and walk, and weep; then they sat, the old man on the wooden chair and the girl on the couch, and listened to the sounds of trees and birds and an occasional car outside the cabin. He picked strengthening plants from the swamp and brewed her tea, fed her sweet venison from a young deer he had shot and dressed just for her. Brought from the woods a snarl of sweetgrass, wet and fragrant, that he showed her how to braid and to coil and stitch into baskets. He noticed that each day she cried a little less.

On a rainy afternoon in late fall, when the cabin had been cleaned until there was nothing left to clean and the furniture rearranged until it had repeated itself four times, she replaced the frayed ribbon trim on his moccasins with a new red ribbon he had bought her for her hair, then lay on the couch, where she fell asleep. She dreamed of flying over Lost Lake, over rice stalks growing a ripe light green up out of water that reflected the sky, the clouds, and Margie overhead; of Zho Wash below walking in the woods, the beaded wild roses on his moccasins scattering petals that took root and bloomed in his path. She awoke to the sound of tiny bells and looked out the window at a storm of ice crystals breaking themselves on the frozen ground outside the cabin. In a small patch of sunlight caused by a break in the clouds above, glittering crystals bulleted from the sky, danced impetuously as they landed, prisms that seized the color of the sun and captured it in the yard outside the cabin, then shattered it against ground frozen hard. She watched the crystals heap and grow, listening to the chiming of the bells that had become menacingly assonant, and began to worry about Zho Wash. Would the truck skid on ice, slide off the road? Would he be hurt? The clouds covered over the sky, the sun set, the woods around the cabin darkened. Would the truck slide off the road? Would it skid; would he be hurt? She put two more pieces of wood in the stove and peeled potatoes that she put on to boil, opened cans of beans and corn. Set two plates, two forks, two coffee cups on the table. Would the truck skid on ice; would he slide off the road and be hurt?

The truck cantered up the driveway.

"It's Zho Wash," she said aloud, and opened the door before he had walked up the steps.

See how pretty it is outside, he had asked. You're home, she had said, then turned her head and dropped the carton of eggs on the floor. Kneeling, sopping up shell and runny egg with Zho, she looked down, hiding the tears that were running off the end of her nose and mixing with the eggs. As they stood to shake the mess from dishcloths into the garbage, she mopped her face with her sweatshirt sleeve, sniffed, and looked away.

"See how pretty it is outside?" he asked again.

She spoke toward the woods. "It looks slippery. You could have gone off the road."

"Margie-enjiss, it's all right. It's all right, Margie; come out on the porch with me, and we'll watch the storm."

~ ~ ~

The winter afternoon that Michael arrived to visit his father, Zho Wash was out in the woods and Margie was in the kitchen, wiping a dishrag over the scarred table that looked as old as the house, she thought, wondering if she should paint it. She heard the door open, turned.

"Michael." The pain was lightning that lit the room with a blue flash and burned flesh from her face and chest, exposing the rawness that was Margie inside. She rasped, "Biindigen, come in. It's good to see you."

"Margie." He had thought she was in Duluth.

When Zho Wash returned, Margie met him at the door. "Look who's here," she said, her voice a semipitch higher than usual. "It's Michael!"

They offered Michael raspberry tea, a comfortable place to sit near the woodstove, and shared their supper of commodity pork and macaroni and cheese. The cabin was tidy; she had hung new curtains, rearranged the furniture. Zho Wash had painted the kitchen shelves, replaced the front stairs.

"Looks nice in here," Michael commented uneasily. What were they, honeymooners? Unnerved, he slept in the shed outside the kitchen, with the dogs. It became his bedroom whenever he visited.

~ ~ ~

She didn't rice the next season. By the end of an unusually humid and hot summer her hands and feet had swelled; her bony ankles that in winter Zho Wash had loved to hold in his hands and tap, cup, caress, were by ricing time lost under the fluid that gravity pulled and held, water finding its own weight. Her abdomen was a wide melon held low to her body by wavy silver stripes of stretch marks; her round face reddened like a tomato even at such light exertions as hanging clothes on the line outside the cabin.

She would have the baby at the allotment house, Margie told Zho Wash; she would not leave Sweetgrass. If she needed help, they would ask Beryl.

She slept on her back, more heavily at night, more soundly; she felt rested and cooled in the mornings, got up to fix breakfast. After the dishes were done and the bed made, she chose one chore for the day, washing the floor or dusting or rearranging the dish cabinet or doing a load of laundry in the wringer washer. During the hottest parts of the afternoons she rested, ready to get off her feet that were rising like bread dough. Lying on the bed with the pictures of Zho Wash's wives for company (one on the table by the bed, one on the wall; Eva young and solemn, Lucy young and laughing), cooled by the fan he had bought at the hardware store in Mesabi and rigged to blow on her feet and legs, never on her face, which bothered her, she stretched her body nearly the entire length of the bed; mysteriously, she was taller lying down than she was standing up. In spite of the heat, and her size, and the swelling and pressure that gave her an occasional nosebleed, she slept lightly away when she lay down in the afternoons, her spine stretched straight and relaxed, the baby moving occasionally but, again mysteriously, content to rest against the uneven boniness of her vertebrae. She loved going to bed while it was light outside; she appreciated the bed's placement under the window, its cool sheets, the man-made breeze from the fan, set on low, blowing slowly across her; the sounds of Zho Wash moving in the yard or the shed, or cutting wood, or cleaning and boiling roots in the kitchen soothed her. Sometimes when she awoke he was next to her, asleep; she never noticed when he lay down because he was so careful to not jar the bed or touch her, respecting her and the baby's rest. His wide mouth smiled in sleep; he snored a light, old man's snore from the back of his throat. One hand, darkened and roughened by sun and work, rested on the edge of her pillowcase.

The afternoon before the baby was born, she woke Zho Wash by kissing that hand and then murmuring her dreams against his lips until he loved her, whispering the name he called her, Margie-enjiss. The next morning she awoke before dawn with the realization that her belly had not moved for hours; frightened, she walked out onto the stoop, where she began to pray. In the black sky overhead, stars sharp as glass glittered remotely; then, as the pink of sunrise faded their brilliance and sent them to their day-time sleep, the baby leapt so high that her nightgown rippled, and she went into labor.

At sunset Zho Wash heated broth on the woodstove for sup-per, put clean sheets on the bed, brewed tea; then they walked in the yard and in the woods around the cabin while they waited.

Margie eased her pains by sitting on the old man's lap, facing him, on a wooden kitchen chair, with her knees drawn up and her feet resting on the chair rungs. He held her with his stringy, mus-cular arms wrapped around and supporting her hips; she rested her head against his chest, just below his shoulder, and was quieted by the beat of his heart. Calmed, she breathed deeply through the pains, inhaling sweetness from the soft brown skin of his neck; as one pain began to grab her, ready to shake her by the hair, she opened her eyes and saw that he was rocking her almost imper-ceptibly, looking out the window at the trees outside the cabin, his lips moving as he prayed all but silently, his hair an unearthly sil-ver under the electric light that hung from the ceiling. "Why, it's Zho," she thought, "it's Zho," and rested her face against the right side of his neck, her lips soft on the line of pale scars, tracks left by the bullet that found him when he was in Italy, during the war.

Crystal left Margie's body under her own force, fists first, hands crossed above her head. She arched her back, twisted, pushed with her tiny feet until she emerged. At first she was gray in color; Zho Wash loosened the cord from where it was wrapped around and around those crossed hands, and her color changed to lavender, then to a deep pink. The cord cut, and free of her mother, she looked coolly at Margie and Zho Wash with eyes the darkest of muddy azure. While Margie held her baby, wrapped as stiffly as a doll, Zho Wash unfolded a new, navy blue bandanna and lay it on the bed. He placed on it a foil bag of Half and Half tobacco, an old solid silver dime, a beaded bracelet, and a ten-dollar bill, then tied the four corners together, opposite corners over opposite corners.

"For when she is named," he explained.

Margie nodded.

"Who will you ask to be her namer?"

"I thought Uncle Earl."

"And what will you call her?"

"Crystal Jo Washington."

Animoosh

1998

THE STRANGER SHOWED UP at the Lost Lake boat landing on opening day of the Mozhay Point Indian Reservation wild rice harvest and stood on the shore next to his ricing car, a forest green Jeep Cherokee with a "Save Our Forests: No Logging" bumper sticker on the rear door, a Che Guevara decal on the driver's side window, and a bicycle mounted upright on the roof. He was dressed for the occasion in an outfit that stood out in the crowd of rice pickers: a new-looking, many-pocketed North Face windbreaker with matching pants tucked into laced Gore-Tex hiking boots, a spotless white mock-turtleneck sweater, and bicycle gloves. He'd donned it that morning thinking about durability and versatility, clothing suitable to wear for an outdoor event new to him, not realizing until he arrived at the landing the incompatibilities of his carefully planned sporting style and the hard and muddy labor of the wild rice harvest. The Mozhay Point wild ricers were wearing jeans, sweatshirts, and running shoes; some had bandannas wrapped around their heads; several wore satin bar-style jackets ("Sanitary Harry's: Where You Can Eat Off the Floor," said one); two old men were tying string around the gathered ankles of their baggy work pants. A young man and woman carried an aluminum canoe past him without appearing to notice him standing there at all, until the young man turned around to quickly double-take the stranger over, up and down, then away.

He smiled widely, although uncertainly, holding out a small card, his Mozhay Point Indian Reservation ricing permit, to the people passing by and asking, too loudly, "Excuse me; is anyone looking for a partner?" There weren't any takers; everyone already had their partners, it appeared, or already knew someone else there who was looking.

Who was the stranger? Indians were pairing up right and left, meeting their cousins, pulling their boats to the shore, pushing off into the water, getting out on the lake. Everybody had a partner except the guy with the Cherokee, the one decked out in the conspicuous ricing outfit. As more people arrived at the landing he raised his voice, called into the void of response, "Is anyone here looking for a partner?" No one answered, no one talked to him, although they were talking to each other, calling out *boozhoo boozhoo how you been* and asking what part of the lake was ready. Kidding around, teasing each other, nobody saying a word to the guy in the sporty ensemble.

But everybody noticed him.

"Looks like he lost the guy who was riding on top of his car."

"Must've been his ricing partner."

"What's he doing with that card?"

"Maybe he's gonna try to charge some rice!"

"Is somebody carding Indians? . . . ay-y-y!"

Everybody was watching the stranger, but nobody looked at him. Everybody was as obviously and surreptitiously curious as Indians can appear, but of course nobody asked the stranger anything. Who was he? Was he a Shinnobi? Was he a white guy, and if he was, how did he get the reservation ricing permit? Would it be proper to ask him where he was from and who his family was, what anybody knows are the polite things to ask at Mozhay? What to do?

The stranger swallowed, continued to show his teeth nervously to the group. Was there anyone in charge, he wondered. Should he ask if there was anywhere to rent a boat?

The ricers appeared to run out of jokes and whispers and started glancing toward an old woman sitting in a webbed lawn chair. As the oldest person at the boat landing (sideways glance), she would know what to do (sideways glance).

Beryl sighed. Ai, the Elders had to do everything, it seemed. She had to come out on opening day before dawn, to stand by Jerome Etienne as he gave the invocation; with Jerome, she had to point out what they had known for how many years of their ricing days, and how many years since that they didn't even go out on the lake anymore, where the pretty, light green places were out there, where the rice would be ready to pick. After the invocation Jerome had disappeared into the back of his son's camper to take a nap, and because getting up so early was harder and harder to do as she got older, Beryl wondered if he felt the same way she did: these younger people, what if Beryl and Jerome told them to start later in the day, and if they wanted to start out so early, let the old people sleep for a while; after all, they had earned it; and then stop asking all those same old questions and just think and remember how they did it last year, and the year before. Before Noel died, the two of them were out there every year since before they got married, and anybody who bothered to pay attention and learn something could have seen how Noel looked out just careful for the color of the rice stalks to get to that pretty green, the way he'd learned it from watching people who'd started ricing long before him. But she had humored them, no point in being unkind, told them that today it would be time. And now here she was, up too early (she had never been able to get back to sleep once she was up) and wishing for her housecoat and television. She could have been home in her trailer, on the couch with her legs up and watching her morning programs; instead, here she was with her tennies getting wet and muddy, sitting on a lawn chair that felt tippy and cut into the backs of her thighs, holding a Styrofoam cup of bad coffee that was going to turn her plate brown for sure so she'd have to scrub it with bleach water tonight, with all these people expecting her to now do something about the strange man in the fancy jacket. Ai. It was always her. She pushed on the chair arms to get to her feet, groaning a little and waving away her nephew's arm. Standing, she leaned on the cane that Noel had used before he died, which sunk into the mud under her weight, annoying her further. *Smile, old lady,* she thought to herself. *No need to be all crabby and* manaadis. She shuffle-clumped slowly toward the stranger, thinking how when she was a young woman, helping Noel push the rowboat out from the shore, she had hopped around like a robin. And climbed into the boat just easy, light and limber as a cat. A person doesn't appreciate that kind of thing until they get older.

Beryl stood next to the stranger. "Hello, young man," she said in her soft *mindemooye* old woman voice that floated, lighter than air, to the lake, where it hovered, dropped into the water, and disappeared.

He stepped to face her directly, closely, blocking the lake. "Good morning!" Such a loud voice; he must be full of coffee. "I wonder if you could help me."

"Ooh, do you need help with something?"

"Yes! I'm new here, and I have a ricing permit."

"(Well, I can see that) Ooh, that's nice."

"And I'm looking for an experienced partner to rice with."

"Mm hmm . . . so, where are you from, then?"

"Duluth. I just moved there from Red Wing. My name's Dag Bjornborg!" He reached out and seized her hand, shook it firmly. Arthritis flashed heat lightning into the joints of her ring finger. "What's yours?"

Sigh. Not his fault he didn't know how to act. "Ooh, that's a nice name . . . who are your mother and dad?" Who named their kid after a dog?

"Well." The man in the eye-catching outfit was aware of the (un)stares of the crowd at the landing and that most people near him, although looking around at the sky, the lake, inside their lunch sacks, were listening intently. "I don't know, actually. I was adopted and raised south of the Cities and named after my grandfather, Dagfinn."

Beryl pictured a Mozhay Point rez dog, big and shaggy, humble and scrappy, swimming through the slough with the help of magical fins, perhaps a Nanaboozhoo trick.

"It's a Norwegian name, but my birth mother was from Mozhay Point. I'm an enrolled member of the band here, but I've never wild riced before. I have a permit from the Reservation Business Committee." He showed her the card.

He was a mixed-blood, for sure, with those eyes and that hair, but now that Beryl took another glance she could see he looked like a lot of people she knew, especially some of those families north of Miskwaa. Who might his mother be? If the Ar-Bee-See gave him a ricing permit, he was a band member; if he was a band member, somebody over in the tribal building knew who his mother was. He probably didn't know how to ask. Was he a Dommage? Probably not a LaForce, not good-looking enough.

"I'm not doing this right." Light hazel eyes looked beseechingly into hers, then away. Not his fault.

Beryl raised her chin, although not her voice, to address the entire group at the landing. "So, who doesn't have a ricing partner?" she asked.

Murmurs. Well, me and Jimminy are partners. I promised Rocky; he should be here pretty soon, him. My mom told me that Henry was gonna be ricing with Baby Al this year.

"Tommy, find somebody who needs a partner, will you? Was Irene ricing today?"

"I think she's ricing with Butch, but you know? Crystal was saying she might be going," somebody said.

"I saw her last night over at Harry's; she was talking about going out today."

"Crystal? Yaa, she was talking about borrowing Michael's boat."

"Well, thank you very much!" Did he have to holler like that? "Where could I find Crystal?"

"Tommy, show him where to find Crystal, will you?" Beryl directed her nephew. "I'm gonna sit here awhile and finish my coffee." She exchanged looks with another old woman and backed up against the lawn chair, grasping its plastic arms and shifting her weight from feet to backside, with a plop. "Sis, nimise," she said, so softly that the crowd couldn't hear, "when are these young people going to learn to do some of these things for themselves?"

"Amanj, Beryl, my girl; who knows?" Sis held out a package of cookies. "Here, have a Fig Newton. Keep you regular."

"Can I take two?"

"Sure, it'll put a smile on your face."

The crowd at the boat landing watched Tommy and the stranger drive down the dirt road and take the curve toward the LaForce family's allotment.

"I never seen a dog drive a car before," somebody commented. The crowd laughed and drifted down the path to the launch.

"I felt kind of sorry for him," commented Sis, pouring more coffee into her and Beryl's cups.

"Niij'kwe, he seems like a young man with a good heart," Beryl answered.

Sis dunked a corner of Fig Newton, nibbled slowly. "And he says he's a Mozhay Pointer; so, who do you think he is?"

As the rice pickers launched canoes and rowboats from the landing, the two old women sipped their coffee and thought.

~ ~ ~

This was too nice to use for a ricing truck, Tommy thought. Where was this guy thinking he would put his rice, if he got any? Everything inside was really clean; a bag of wild rice picked right out of the lake and dragged across the ground would get the seats and the carpets wet and muddy. The stranger didn't know to bring any plastic bags, or a tarp. He hoped Crystal was home at Beryl's; otherwise, Beryl would make Tommy rice with the stranger, he just knew it. Brooding, he almost forgot to tell the stranger which mailbox was Beryl's.

"Turn in right here; that's where she lives," he instructed.

The stranger braked and cut the wheel fast; the Cherokee squealed off the blacktop and onto the dirt driveway, cutting a neat crescent around the pink mailbox on a green-painted sawhorse twined with pink plastic roses. By dumb luck they missed and overshot the young woman walking out onto the road from Beryl's, raising dust from the driveway. The stranger broke into a sweat. "Oh, God," he said.

She looked up and glared, shading her eyes.

Tommy stuck his head out of the window and asked, "Crystal, you going ricing today?"

She had a long, straight-legged stride and broad shoulders that swung with her steps, and was so short she stood on tiptoe to peer into the vehicle, gripping the door with both hands on the bottom of the window, where her chin rested. The front of her shirt and pants would carry the road dust from where she leaned her skinny body in its baggy clothes against the door; she wouldn't bother to brush it off. She took a drag on her cigarette and coughed before she answered, "If I find a partner." Her peculiarly brown-blue eyes were narrow in her round face, and she looked tired.

"This is Dog, here, and he's looking for a partner with a boat."

"Happy to meet you, Crystal!" Dag reached across Tommy and through the window to grab her hand firmly and pumped, like that man visiting the tribal center from the state college, that recruiter.

"Hey, uh, pleased to meet you, too, uh . . . what was his name?"

"It's Dog," said Tommy. "So, you going ricing today, or what? Dog, here, is looking for an experienced ricing partner."

"That's me . . . ay-y-y!" answered Crystal, and the three laughed, Dag not sure why.

"I was gonna take Zho Wash's old rowboat; my mom said he wouldn't care. And the knockers, too. And Michael's duckbill." She coughed again, craned her head inside the window to get a better look at Dag, narrowed her eyes further and rasped, "Hey. He ever rice before?"

"I haven't, Crystal, but I'm here to learn!"

Well, he seemed pretty wide-awake, anyway. "You got coffee in there?"

"A six-pack of Coke, and I've brought along some sandwiches from Duluth."

A suspicious look from Crystal.

"Subways."

"Anything else?"

"M&M cookies."

"Can I wear your sunglasses?"

"Uh, sure, you can wear them."

"You got any aspirin?"

"I have Motrin and some generic aspirin-free pain reliever . . ."

"Well. All right. Let's go get the rowboat." Crystal opened the back door and hopped up to swing her backside into the rear seat; she misjudged the distance. Her hip bounced against the seat and slammed her other side against the open door. Back on the ground, she kept her balance by throwing her arms wide, hit one against the door, muttered "shit," and climbed, more slowly on the second try, up to the seat. "Let's maajaa, Animoosh. Can I have a couple aspirin and one of those Cokes?"

They backtracked toward Lost Lake and turned into another driveway, this one nearly covered by a sumac stand and marked by a large, rusting mailbox with "Joseph Washington" painted in peeling letters on the side. The driveway was a leaf-covered tunnel; at the end, the house looked closed up, abandoned, yet there was laundry clipped to a line hung between the house and a rusting spruce.

"Quiet in here; Michael must have took the dogs with him," said Tommy.

"Good thing," Crystal answered.

They found the rowboat behind the shed, the duckbill pole and knocker sticks under the porch. After moving the bicycle to inside the Jeep, Dog and Tommy tied the rowboat, pole, and sticks onto the roof rack. Crystal went back into the shed and came out carrying a canvas tarp and a bundle of gunnysacks, which she set carefully on the ground while she helped herself to a dish towel from the clothesline and tied her hair into a turban. She looked more tired than before she'd had the caffeine; the lines from her nose to the corners of her mouth were deeper than Aunt Beryl's, her face pale and puffy. Looks a little like death warmed over, thought Tommy. "You feeling all right, Crystal?"

She braced one arm against the back door and held the other, full of gunnysacks, to her chest as she coughed, nodding her head, yes.

The stranger looked concerned. "She's a pretty good ricer," Tommy whispered to him. "She just needs a partner."

~ ~ ~

Dag and Crystal had been out in the rowboat for nearly an hour, and Dag thought that Tommy was right, she seemed to know what to do. She had spread the tarp out on the floor of the rowboat, piled the gunnysacks under the seats, carefully. While cautioning Dag to not kick the sacks under the seats with his heavy boots she had helped push the boat down the launch. She had told him how to pole from the back of the rowboat, pushing away with the duckbill while she bent the rice stalks over into the boat with the knockers, right knock-knock, left knock-knock, raining hulls onto the tarp on the floor in front of her.

She was a hard worker, Dag thought, although she didn't seem much for conversation. She answered his comments about the weather and the size of the lake, and what the weather had been like when he'd left Duluth, with "mm's" and "mm hmm's"; other than that she hadn't said a word since they arrived at the landing except to give him directions. Dag finally had no choice but to be quiet and get used to working without conversation. He concentrated on pushing the boat forward smoothly with his pole, taking care to give Crystal time enough to bend and tap the rice stalks, right knock-knock, left knock-knock, before moving on, slowing when she slowed, speeding up when she did, matching his motions to hers. Physically, the work was as demanding as he had expected it to be; the technique was more difficult, but he enjoyed the rhythm of working with Crystal. Under her loose plaid shirt her body moved from side to side as her arms lifted, right knock-knock, left knock-knock, and her rather stately turbaned head moved gracefully as if to a tune, her straight back a metronome while her hips lifted slightly from the bench side to side, shoulders swaying, arms lifting, right knock-knock, left knock-knock. Arms, shoulders, back, hips. Right knock-knock, left knock-knock. A steady rhythm of work broken only by Crystal's coughing attacks.

He tired before she did. "Crystal, do you think it's time for lunch?" She stopped and turned around to look at him through his too-big sunglasses, nodded, and brushed insects and leaves from her arms and lap. Dag pulled up the pole and laid it carefully the length of the boat, then opened the cooler. "Would you like a Spicy Italian?" he asked politely.

After a fit of coughing rough enough to bend her nearly in half, with her arms crossed across her stomach, Crystal felt an appetite coming on. She cleared her throat, took an M&M cookie out of the bag, ate it in two bites, and took a couple of deep breaths.

"My girlfriend went out with one once," she answered, feeling a little better now that her hangover was beginning to wear off. "So, are you Italian, or what?"

After the silent morning it took Dag a second to catch on; then he laughed.

"I'm a member of the Mozhay Point Band of Ojibwe."

"Yeah, but what else? Where are you from?"

"Well." How to begin? "I don't really know. I was born in Duluth, and right after that I was adopted."

"Ooh, you were adopted out." One of many thousands, each with a wishful and searching story, which was probably what brought this one to Mozhay.

"I was raised in Red Wing—know where that is, between Minneapolis and Rochester?—and moved to Duluth last spring. My birth mother was from Mozhay Point. I don't know who she was, but I was put on the tribal rolls when I was born. I've never been to Mozhay Point before, though; I've never been north of Duluth until today."

"Ooh." She didn't say anything more.

Dag and Crystal ate, Crystal smoked and coughed, and between coughs they sat in the rowboat listening to the sounds of boats being poled through the lake, through tall wild rice stalks, and rice pickers talking and laughing. "Whoa, whoa, whoa, look out; don't tip us over," a man's voice called softly, urgently. His partner, a woman, answered, "Just got to stand and stretch. Don't you worry, now; I never tipped anybody over yet." They laughed.

Crystal slid off the rowboat bench and rested her head against the cooler. She crossed her arms over her eyes and reclined under the sun, in the rowboat with Dag, surrounded by tall, pale green wild rice stalks. The stalks made a wall around them, and although they could hear other people talking and laughing on the lake, they couldn't see anything through the wall of rice. It was like a room without doors or windows, a green room, Dag thought, with a blue ceiling.

The people in the next boat left, the boat sliding through ripe rice with a swishing, rippling sound; then there was silence. Crystal's jaw and mouth slackened, loosened; then she swallowed and her wide mouth tightened and lifted at the corners into a near smile. Was she sleeping, Dag wondered. Should he ask? He took another Coke out of the cooler and turned from the girl, in order to not wake her with the sound of the can opening, and watched her sleep while he drank.

Crystal, Crystal. Who are you; who might you be? Who might I be? he thought.

She slid down from the cooler into a small, broad-shouldered puddle of hungover Indian girl on the bottom of the rowboat.

Might our lives have crossed before, Crystal? Might they ever cross again after today? Her chest rose and fell as she breathed slowly and deeply; barely rising from her unbuttoned flannel shirt her breasts, flattened in sleep, were two shallow mysteries of soft flesh covered by the lumpiness of a wrinkled, too-large brassiere and T-shirt. Watching her, Dag breathed with the rise and fall of Crystal's chest, succumbing to a rhythm that nearly pulled him into sleep; then his head jerked. Up, wake up.

"Crystal?"

She turned onto her side, coughed twice in her sleep, and pulled her flannel shirt over her ear. Dag's sunglasses, scuba goggles on her small, wide face, were knocked crooked.

Crystal. You're on the short side, like me. What does your mother look like; is she short, too? I was watching you while you worked; you have good arms, strong. Is that from ricing? Do you do other hard work, too? I look at you, and I look at the other Indians at the boat landing, and it's pretty obvious that none of you think that I might belong here, too. I have my enrollment card for Mozhay Point Reservation; they gave me a ricing permit when I applied for one. I'm legally enrolled; I probably have more Indian blood in me than some of the people at the boat landing who wouldn't talk to me. I don't know much about Indians or my birth parents, or anything else. When I look at you I can see how like the other people at the boat launch you are: you all know each other, and you know things about each other that you've known since you were born, some things you wish you didn't know, probably, but you know who you are. And you just take that for granted; you don't know how lucky you are, and you treat me as if I don't know some big secret that the rest of you do. You're right, I don't know it. If I knew it, I'd be like you.

I have a memory of a stroller with a canopy, my mother pushing me down the street and stopping at a neighbor's yard. "He's so lucky," the neighbor said, bending to look below the canopy. "Just think of the life he would be living if it wasn't for you. And he doesn't look Indian at all."

Just look at my teeth; my mother took me to the dentist twice a year. I brushed them twice a day. I wore braces to fix an overbite. Look at them. They're whole and white and straight, the best set of any on the entire boat landing. When I got acne, my mother took me to a dermatologist. When my clothes wore out, or when I outgrew them, or when they went out of style, I got new ones. When I outgrew my bike, I got a bigger one. When things needed fixing, they got fixed. I was a Cub Scout. When my mother took me shopping in the Cities for new school clothes, I would see them, the real Indians is how I thought of them, sitting on the steps of apartment buildings, or wandering around as if they had all the time in the world, or sometimes drunk and staggering or even sleeping on the sidewalk, and I would wish I could get closer, look at their faces, hoping someone would look back, that someone would know me. That woman, are my eyes like hers, I would wonder, or that man, do my shoulders hang like his?

Are we related, Crystal-short-like-me? If we were, wouldn't we somehow be able to recognize one another; wouldn't there be some type of bond stronger than the circumstances of our absence from one another, strong enough that we would just know?

Crystal. How old are you? I never dated any Indian girls. How would I ever have met any, and where? At Hi-Y? DeMolay? And how could I have explained to my parents, to my friends, if I had wanted to take one of the Prairie Island girls, a girl like you, to the movies, to the prom?

"How about you, Crystal? Did you get to the prom?"

"Huh? Wegonen? What's that, Animoosh?" Crystal sat up.

"Sorry, I must have been thinking out loud. Is it time to get to work?"

"Sure, let's work. Anookii-daa. You want to try knocking for a while?"

The rowboat rocked as Dag stood to change places with Crystal. She said, "Down, get down. Don't stand in the boat." Dag knelt. "OK, now you just crawl to the bench, here, and I'll step over you; I'm lighter than you, so the boat won't lean so much under me."

The changing of places was like a choreographed performance, Dag thought. We might be ballet dancers, or figure skaters, Crystal light as a bird and me ready to lift her to the sky. As she passed over his shoulder, the heady combination that made up Crystal became to Dag a body-heated breeze, moving air a fragrance of strength and thinness, muscles and fragility, an irresistible bouquet that turned his head; that soft part of Crystal below her armpit and on a level with her left breast brushed Dag's face, which turned farther, nearly making contact with that breast, so lightly that she appeared to not feel it at all. He stopped her with a hand at her waist and with the other pulled off the sunglasses, placed them in his jacket pocket, pulled the turban off her head, grasped her hair and twisted, winding it twice around his fingers so that his hand was wrapped in hair and bound tightly against the back of her head, pulling. Crystal's face was tipped up toward Dag's, her eyes open wide and slanting, creases smoothed by the pressure of his hand pulling that tail of hair back and down. She stared, mouth open, one arm pinned against her ribs, the other holding her cigarette out to the side. Dag pulled her closer with one hand, thinking, she has a waist under that big shirt, touched by her slightness and softness. He pictured an unknown, mysterious Indian brave with long black hair and brown arms, hard and muscular, who held Crystal's slenderness against his rocklike warrior strength, his hawklike face nearly brutal in its pride and survival, its Indian-ness, crushing to his burnished copper chest a nearly breathless, swooning, succumbing Crystal.

The generic Indian brave, who was Dag, closed his eyes and kissed Crystal, who had become an Indian princess, against an imaginary, impossibly brilliant pink and gold sunset.

She tasted like cigarettes and coffee, pickles and salami, and also ever so vaguely of a sweet vomit. Earth, the brave told himself, it was the taste of the earth, and of ceremonial smoke. The princess was still, unmoving, transfixed in the moment, the timelessness and sheer beauty of smooth lips and wild hearts under an impressionist painting of sunset created by Mother Earth herself.

Crystal didn't move but waited, her lips rough and cool, the creases of her face smoothed and her eyes wide open and slanted by the pressure of his hand pulling her hair back and down, and waited, looking right through Dag to take in the sky as she waited for Dag to stop.

The brave bent his head over that of the conquered princess, blocking the sun and looking deeply into her eyes, as deep muddy blue as the waters of Lost Lake, and transfixed, conquered by the thrill of the forced kiss; then, behind the waiting stillness of Crystal's eyes a shadow moved, and then another.

She remembered her cigarette, held out to the side, probably ashing away into the water, and wished for a drag. "Ow, my hair," she said.

"That's the Indian boy in me." The brave bent over the princess, ready to kiss her again, to kiss Crystal back into that nearly breathless, swooning, succumbing royal forest maiden he had imagined before the reality of the shadows emerged and moved, moved.

Crystal looked into Dag's eyes, then rolled hers. "Animoosh," she said and looked back into the sky. And in that second he heard as clearly as if she'd said it aloud, "Not any Indians I know."

She didn't say, Do you think Indian men chase us around and grab us and pull us by the hair, do you think they do that? You, there, in the fancy outfit, you, there, with the yuppie environmentalist big-bucks car, you think some Indian woman is going to follow you home when she reads your white-guy love medicine bumper stickers? Pretty impressive, advertising yourself with your car. How are sales? Who do you think you are, anyway? She didn't say any of those things. Dag wondered if she thought them, or if he did, himself.

Who did he think he was, she wanted to know. And who was Crystal, this woman who was short like him, this woman who he imagined now wore his face, if he hadn't had a dermatologist, and his overbite, if he hadn't had an orthodontist?

As Dag let go of Crystal's hair, his intended words of apology were overridden by his blurting, "You could be my sister."

"Christ." She sat, bent to paw through the pile of gunnysacks until she found the bottle. "Gawd." She unscrewed the cap, her cigarette still between her second and third fingers, and took a drink. "Here."

"No, thanks. Why would you bring that on the boat?"

"Keeps my stomach down; gets me through the day, Animoosh." She sipped, coughed, noticed her cigarette had burned down, pulled another out of her back pocket and lit it. "How about you? What gets you through the day? Granola? Cappuccino? Your blonde girlfriend? Is her name Tiffany? No, wait; is it Brittany?"

"Allison."

Crystal snorted. "Good thing she's not here."

"I'm sorry, Crystal, I really am. And not just because of Allison; I don't have any excuses. I'm sorry, and I promise that I won't do that again."

"And I'm not your sister. Jesus." Crystal took another sip. "What would ever make you say that? Jeez." She again offered the bottle to Dag.

"I said no thanks. What is that, gin? You'll make yourself sick."

"I don't drink gin; it'll rot your guts. This is vodka. On a full stomach. You don't get sick on that." She offered the bottle again. "Here. Come on, don't make me drink alone."

"I said no thanks." Dag stood again, at the back of the rowboat. "Let's go; I'll pole and you just keep knocking."

"Come on. Michael won't even know we drank it; he wouldn't care if he did. When he's drinking he hides bottles all over the place, just like his old man did; forgot where he put them, most of the time."

"Is Michael your father?"

She paused, pondering, and sipped. "Just somebody with a duckbill. He's married to one of my mom's friends." Cleared her throat. "Here, drink this with me."

"Come on; let's go, Crystal."

"Give me a minute."

"Let's go."

"Forget it, Animoosh. Quit your barking! You can't rice without somebody knocking, and I'm not gonna do it, and so you might as well just settle down." Crystal slid off the bench and lay again in the bottom of the boat, this time with her head on the empty gunnysacks. "I got a headache, I got a hangover, I feel like shit, and I had to listen to you when I was trying to sleep. I had to borrow the goddamn boat, and the pole, and the knockers; I had to show you what to do. And now I'm gonna take a goddamn break here so you might as well get used to it and sit down." She got up on one elbow for another slug of vodka, coughed. "I mean it, Animoosh."

Dag sat. "What's an animoosh? Is it something like Kimosabe? Like the Lone Ranger and Tonto?"

"It's a dog. Get it? Like your name? An animoosh is a dog. Where'd you get that name, anyway?"

"I was named after my grandfather. His full name is Dagfinn."

"Dog Fin? What is he, a Sioux?" Crystal laughed so hard that she hit her head on the side of the boat. "Ow."

"You're a comedian, all right. He's a Norwegian." I'll wait, he thought. I'll wait until she falls asleep; then I'll use the oars and try to row back. Which way is the landing?

The lake was nearly silent. Dag listened to the breeze moving and rice stalks rustling. Crystal took off her shoes, dug her forearm across the bridge of her nose, over her eyes. Her body twitched and jerked as she dove for sleep, grew slack, then stiff as she turned to her side, drew her knees into the fetal position, back curled and tight, elbows squeezed to ribs, hands up and supplicating in fists that held tight to the back collar of unconsciousness. She squinted against the white light of the sun that was a red heat back of her eyelids, her struggle catatonic. Dag bent to pick up the dish towel, draped it over her eyes. Her breath, and the heat that rose from her body, smelled stale and tired, restless. Cigarette smoke damp on a pair of unwashed jeans. Liquor bleeding through pores, absorbed into a too-big T-shirt and a limp flannel shirt. Crystal inhaled and exhaled deeply, painfully, her very diaphragm part of the struggle, forcing warm ricing-time air in, out, in, out, an ironclad lung. She frowned, squinted, farted. Muttered. Opened her eyes. "Who the fuck are you?" she asked, and fell back asleep.

He gave it two more minutes, timed on his watch. "Crystal?" he whispered, and reached for the oars, which were locked. Dag stood, balanced his weight with one foot on each side of the sleeping young woman. His shadow, cast across her eyes, blocked out the sun, and the red back of her eyelids shaded to a cool purple. Her vodka dreams, those flights through long grass that waved in a still and windless vacuum, grasping her ankles with bladed and twining fingers that tore at their roots in the earth as she ran, while the foul and ravenous breath of the Windigo behind her steamed and burned her back, causing her hair to fall out and into the cannibal's ravenous path, those dreams in Dag's shadow became an ice age, ten thousand years that she ran through a dark and frozen forest, barefoot on frost-covered rocks, slipping, startled awake, to behold Dag, who had shifted his weight to his right foot in order to unlock the oar, and who was now stumbling frantically, futilely, to right the rowboat.

"The rice! Jump! Save the rice!" Crystal shouted, as Dag's weight pulled the boat farther to its side. And then Crystal took a deep breath as she, along with the cooler, Subway bag, bottle of vodka, the sacks, pole, knockers, and the rice slid into the lake after Dag, and the boat filled with water and sank.

Crystal surfaced, treading water. "Help!" she shouted, "Help!" She felt for the boat with her feet, found it, balanced and stood. She gasped, coughed, breathed. "Help!" she shouted again. "We tipped over!"

A man's voice called back, "Coming over, keep hollering; we'll find you!"

"Here . . . here, we're over here!" Where was Dag?

Dag kicked against the arms of lake weeds that pulled him

down, down to the mud at the bottom of the lake. He pushed against their fluid and sinewy grasp with arms that became further entangled, then unable to move. I want to see the sun, he thought, before I die, and opened his eyes to find it, pale yellow and wavering through the lake surface, not too far above the dark watery green and black of weeds and rice. Allison, he thought. If there is life after death, a thousand years from now I will tell you every day about the sun I saw through the lake, from the bottom of the lake, the sun the color of your hair, the sight and the thought of you the very last I had in this life.

When he stopped struggling and gave in to death, the weeds loosened their hold on his ankles, and he was able to stand with his feet on the slick mud of the lake bottom and his face at the surface. He vomited water, slipped, and felt a hand pass across his left ear, across his face. "Right in back of you, I'm standing on the rowboat, Dag." He stood again, pushed with his feet toward the voice. Crystal grasped the neck of his shirt. "Hang on to me. Stand on the boat." Crystal was treading water, bobbing up and down on top of the sunken rowboat. "Somebody's coming, Dag." They locked wrists and alternated bobbing on top of the boat, pulling each other back when they slipped off, buoyant acrobats in an underwater stunt. "Here, we're over here," Crystal called each time the man's voice asked, "You see us yet?"

They were separated by the ricers, a burly young longhair and his father, who directed Crystal and Dag to each hold to one side of their canoe, which they paddled through the rice stalks and weeds back to shore. The old man and Dag were silent, one with the perspective of his years and the other with the exhaustion and perspective of his day. Crystal and the longhair, however, conversed. Briefly.

"Lake got all your rice, eh? How much did youse have?"

"Not so much. Good for next year's rice." She glared across the canoe at Dag.

"Hey, we'll have to make sure we remember that spot next year!" the longhair laughed. "Lots of good rice there!"

Silence from Crystal.

"How did you tip a rowboat over?" the longhair asked.

Silence from Crystal.

"It was my fault. I stood up to take the oars," said Dag.

Silence from the longhair, and a snort.

The old man spoke. "Hey, didn't Zho Wash do that, that one time? Tipped over the rowboat, all his rice went into the lake, remember that? Tried to act all Indianish: 'It was meant to be,' he said, but oh, you could tell he was mad, though!" The two men in the canoe began to tell all of the stories they could remember about people tipping their boats and losing their rice in the lake, each funnier to them than the last, by what Dag heard, but not a single one funny to him. Why in the world had he even come to Lost Lake? What made him think he could rice? He had checked a video out of the county historical society's library, watched old film footage of it done by people who were probably dead long before he was born, people who could possibly have been his grandparents, closely watching the faces of the man in the overalls and the woman in the housedress and straw hat as they glided in a canoe through the tall plants on the lake, the man poling, the woman tapping precious heads from ripened rice stalks into the boat, working in tandem expertly, effortlessly, with the practice of generations before them. Thought, this is where I come from, this is my home, this is the goodness and simplicity and the beauty of my home. My home.

Closer to shore the lake became shallow enough for Dag and Crystal to let go of the canoe and walk onto the landing, where the crowd of people, cooking, eating, hoisting sacks of green rice into their cars and trucks, began to ask what happened. Crystal, who still hadn't directed a word toward Dag since they were rescued by the men in the canoe, angrily answered, "nothing," which caused laughter. She shook her head no to Tommy's offer of a ride back to Beryl's and walked with that long, short-legged, fast stride away from Dag, past the Cherokee, away from the crowd, toward the road.

"Crystal. Crystal, wait." She slowed, her back to him. "Crystal, you saved my life."

"Why didn't you jump off the boat? Christ, we didn't just lose the rice, somebody's got to go back and try to get the boat out and try to find the oars, and the pole, and the knockers are probably gone, that's for sure. And my shoes. You already almost tipped it over once; didn't you learn anything? Christ, why didn't you jump off the boat?" She walked faster.

"I'm sorry, Crystal; I just didn't think. I haven't done this before."

"Forget it, just forget it." She kept walking.

"Crystal, I'm sorry. I'll help, and I'll buy you some new shoes."

"Just leave me alone." She was at the road and needed to raise her voice. "Leave me alone!" Barefoot she walked down the road, away from Dag, with that long, short-legged stride.

"He's sorry," she mumbled to herself. "Sorry, sorry, sorry."

The keys to the Cherokee were still zipped in his windbreaker pocket. Ignored, it seemed, by the crowd, he walked back toward the Jeep, past the old women in the lawn chairs.

"Well, what do we think, old lady?" Sis pointed with her chin toward the new rice picker as he passed. Beryl turned her head to call directly to him, in her soft *mindemooye* voice that floated, lighter than air, "Young man."

And again, "Young man." That soft *mindemooye* voice floated, lighter than air, across Dag's face and chest, branding the moment into his memory and his heart, then into the sky over Mozhay Point, where it hovered and became the gentlest of rains.

"Would you like to know who your mother is?"

The Ar-Bee-See

1998

AFTER HENRY AND BABY AL FISHED THEM out of the lake, Crystal and that poor young man with the funny name and the fancy ricing clothes, both of them soaking wet and Crystal without any shoes, walked away from the boat landing and past the row of chairs where Sis and me were waiting for a ride home.

"My, my, Beryl; do you see that?" Sis asked.

We could see that Crystal was having nothing nice to do with Dog Fin; she walked away fast, just fa-a-ast, yelling at him, and headed toward Sweetgrass; shoulders all hunched, he walked past us looking just plain beaten down. But Sis and I had been thinking and talking, and his life was about to change.

"Young man," I asked, "would you like to know who your mother is?"

It stopped him in his tracks. He turned around and stared with those light hazel eyes so wide and round they looked just like marbles, then dropped to his knees right in front of me and then rolled down even farther so that he was sitting on his feet. I thought he might next just plain curl up in a little ball. "What did you say?" he asked.

Five minutes later he had moved his bike from the inside of the station wagon to back up on the roof again, and packed me in the front seat and Sis along with our lawn chairs and lunch buckets in the back. As we rode away from Sweetgrass and toward the Dionne Fork and the Ar-Bee-See building we passed Crystal, who was talking to herself and so didn't see us waving hello. What a ride we had! The car was so tall and so comfortable: for one thing it had bucket seats in front that you could raise up or lower down just with the touch of a button. I set mine as high as I could and so was able to have a whole new look at that part of Mozhay. In fact, when we got to the fork we could have seen right into the Dionne house if Grace had kept her drapes open. It was a shame that nobody seemed to be home and also too bad that Sis was so busy folding and unfolding the back seat and commenting on the carpeting and how the interior was so tall she could practically stand up if she wanted that she didn't even get a good look at the view. Oh, it really was a pleasure to ride in that car, and I was, to tell the truth, a little sorry when we got there and we had to get out. I half wished I had been riding on that bicycle that Dog Fin had tied to the roof.

~ ~ ~

At the RBC Dag all but lifted the two old ladies out of the car and all but carried them up the sidewalk and into the front door. He was pale and short of breath, in near danger of hyperventilating. The receptionist, who was sitting at the front desk, looked concerned.

"Has there been an accident? she asked, picking up the telephone receiver.

"Boozhoo, Merrilee," Beryl answered. "Nooooo, everything is fine. Aneen ezhii ya yayaan?"

"Maybe he better sit down." What in the world had happened to that new ricer? She was about to ask what was going on, then realized that clearly Beryl expected her to remember her manners. "Oh, mino mino mino, niin. How are you, Auntie Beryl? Auntie Sis?"

"We're good, too, Merrilee. How is your mother?"

"Yes, how is Theresa, and how is your dad? This here is Dog Fin; he was out ricing today. He got his permit from somebody here at the Ar-Bee-See."

"That was me; I issued the permit. Good to see you again, Dagfinn. Everything go all right out there?" She smiled fetchingly; maybe the Merrilee/Theresa *jiibik* would work and he would tell her what had happened.

"It's a long story, but yes, everything is all right."

"We're here to help Dog out with the rest of his ricing paperwork. He needs to look at his enrollment records and his birth certificate," said Sis.

"You won't need anything more, just your permit if you sell your rice to Manoominike; that's the tribe's broker," Merrilee told Dag.

Sis tried a firmer approach. "He needs those other records, too; he's thinking of getting married, and he'll need that stuff to enroll his kids. He'll just take copies today and get the originals some other time."

"Those records are sealed in an envelope in his file," Merrilee answered. "They're always kept locked up. That's required by *law.*"

"Are they in that file cabinet?" Sis wanted to know.

"Merrilee, do you have the key?" Beryl asked.

People couldn't just come in and look at files. Nobody could, not even Merrilee. It was the *law.*

"Can't *he* take a look?" asked Sis. "They're *his* records."

Merrilee could tell them that there was really nothing to see. Only the Tribal Council could authorize even letting anybody know if there even was a file, and even if she could get out the file, only his blood quantum information and legal name were viewable, on an affidavit signed by a judge in 1970; Dag already had a copy of it. That same judge had signed across the sealed envelope. His birth certificate might be in there, or it might not, but Merrilee couldn't tell them anything about that because she didn't know: the envelope could be opened only with a court order and by request and permission of the birth mother. It was the *law*.

"Well, what if his mother doesn't know who he is? What if she doesn't know his name? How's she supposed to do that, then?" demanded Sis. "Can you tell us that?"

"Oh, Auntie Sis." Merrilee, who on occasion rather enjoyed a recreational street fight, stood and stepped out from behind the desk; her fetching smile broadened and Beryl thought, *This young woman is built like a weight lifter.* "You know I can't do anything to break the law. It's my *job*."

Sis put her hands on her hips. "Why don't you just help him? Isn't *that* your job? What do you get paid to do here, anyhow?"

Beryl placed a hand on Merrilee's wrist, "My, that is a pretty bracelet. Did your mother make it?" Thinking, *She looks like she could knock me down in two seconds flat,* she put on her voice of reason. "My girl, why don't you just let Dag look in his own envelope? After all, it's his mother."

"Auntie, you know I can't do that."

"Please, Merrilee; if you'll just let me look I promise I won't bother her." Dag was by this time leaning against the desk, begging. His sleeves dragged paintbrush strokes of muddy tracks across the blotter.

"I'm sorry; I really am." She tried a Merrilee/Theresa magic smile again, but Dag didn't respond. His entreating eyes were locked on hers, unblinking. "You'll have to get a court order. I can't do it. You need to talk to your tribal council representative, the one for the Sweetgrass district."

Sis had arrived at the end of her fuse. "To Michael? You want us to talk to *Michael*? That *politician*? Like your dad is going to listen to us when his own daughter is against us? There's corruption right there. Nepotism, it's called. And *that*, my dear, is also against the law!" Sis tapped her fingers on the desk. "Let me talk to my cousin's boy. Is he here? Peanut!"

Merrilee, wanting no trouble with her boss, took a deep breath. "Auntie, I'm going to see if I can find him. Hold on; I promise I'll be right back." Merrilee left the room. Sis reached for the file cabinet by the desk and pulled a drawer open; Merrilee heard the sound of metal rollers, skipped athletically back and closed the drawer. Then she pushed the lock button on the filing cabinet.

Sis raised her voice. "Peanut! Peanut! Help! Help!" and Jack Minogeezhik, tribal chairman of the Mozhay Point Band of Ojibwe, ran out from his office at the back of the building and down the hall to the reception desk.

"Right here! Right here! What's going on?" The sight of bedraggled and shocked Dag drew the same reaction from the chairman as it had from Merrilee. "Has there been an accident?"

"Big accident! That girl almost broke my hand in the file cabinet!"

"You better sit down, Sis," Beryl directed. "Maybe just a little ice. Maybe we won't have to call the tribal police or an ambulance."

Merrilee apologized. "Auntie, I am so sorry. I didn't even see your poor hand. Come with me; come to the break room and I'll make an ice pack."

"Well, maybe it isn't exactly broken but somebody better take a look at it. And my knees are shaking; just look, can you see that?"

"Let's let Merrilee take care of you," said Beryl, "and I'll come with. Peanut, this is Dog, a band member. Dog, how about you stay here with Peanut and tell him what the trouble is."

The three women left, Merrilee supporting Sis with one arm around her waist and the other holding Sis's elbow and hand. Beryl followed, turning with a backward look and nod addressed to the chairman.

The men shook hands, and Dag began to talk.

Another sad story of an adopted-out Indian baby, thought Jack. From after the Second World War until 1978 the government promoted the removal of babies from their mothers and their adoption by white families that would bring them up and assimilate them into the American melting pot. Dag wasn't the first to come to the tribal building looking for his family, his identity, and his birthright, and he wouldn't be the last. He was, however, one of the rare few to have legal status in a band, which meant that he had relatives who knew of his existence and had had the presence of mind, tenacity, and unusual luck to take care of his enrollment. Jack asked Dag what he knew about himself. Dag answered in a low voice hoarse with hope.

Duluth

St. Louis County

Private adoption

Red Wing

the Bjornborgs knew his birth father, somehow

his birth father was a college student in Chicago

August 14, 1971

nothing else; nothing else

Dag sniffed, wiped his nose with his damp jacket sleeve, and walked to the front door. He realized that the Cherokee was ridiculously large for one person, used too much gas, and that Che Guevera didn't look like a Mozhay Point Indian at all. In the front window of the house across the street, closed curtains rippled, swayed, and opened; a scowling wraith leaned forward with crossed arms to peer at the Cherokee. He lifted a hand in greeting; ancient Mrs. Dionne hobbled to one side of the window, pulled a cord, and the drapes closed. He thought he would weep. "I think I might have some grit from the lake in my eyes, and it's bothering my contacts," he said to the chairman. "I'll be right back."

In the men's room he removed his left contact and rinsed it under the faucet, losing it down the sink drain. Sighing, he unzipped one of the half-dozen pockets inside his windbreaker and took a pair of glasses out of a case. Looking in the mirror he fitted them, loose and in need of adjustment, onto the oddly comic face of a stranger who wiggled his eyebrows sadly. Perhaps, after all, Woody Allen was his father and Cher his mother.

Late summer in 1971. A college student in Chicago. Jack pondered. Vietnam, his unanswered letter. Dale Ann's vow of chastity. Dale Ann's love of children. Dale Ann's avoidance of him. Dale Ann.

Dag emerged from the men's room pushing a pair of heavy and rather crooked glasses higher up his long nose that Jack realized resembled Dale Ann's.

"I'll open the envelope. You sit here at the desk. Don't say anything; the ladies in the lunchroom don't need to hear."

~ ~ ~

"Beryl, do you hear a car?" Sis addressed the question to me while Merrilee tenderly iced her hand.

Listening for a motor, Merrilee tipped an ear toward the parking lot as Sis, always very quick on her feet, got out to the front doors of the Ar-Bee-See in time to see Jack and Dag headed toward Lost Lake.

"Well!" said Merrilee.

"Stranded," said Sis, "we're stranded here. Now you're gonna have to give us a ride home, Merrilee. Where are they going?"

I thought it had to be to Sweetgrass to talk to Margie, who was the only one Dale Ann might have told. "Let's call Grace," I suggested. "See if she wants to come over to the Ar-Bee-See for some tea."

Niiwin: Migwechiwendam

Enchanted Agwaching

2008

CRYSTAL SAT WITH HER HANDS FOLDED together at the top of her belly, feet flat on the floor pushing the rocking chair. Floorboards on the recently refinished wooden floor creaked slightly as the chair rocked back and forward. Margie, standing in the doorway, listened with pleasure to the sound. She remembered sitting in that same rocking chair, which Zho Wash had pulled out to the porch that was now half of the combined front room and sunroom, right about where the chair sat now, rocking baby Crystal as she nursed. She had sat with one leg bent under her body, with her foot hooked behind the other knee, and braced the arm that was holding the baby on the chair arm. In those days the floorboards, rough and in need of sanding and varnish, had groaned and sung under the rockers.

The creaking of the chair annoyed Crystal, who wondered if the sound was caused by her weight. She stopped, lifted one foot, made a face. "Look at that; look at how fat my feet are getting."

"Put them up; that's just water, not fat. Here." Margie pulled a wooden crate up to the rocker, and lifted her daughter's feet onto it. "Putting them up will help." Crystal's feet were getting awfully swollen, she thought. They looked puffy and soft, and her toes stuck out as round and hard as grapes. "Did you paint your toenails yourself, or did Dagfinn?"

"Now, can you picture me letting Dag paint my toenails when you know how much I hate anybody touching my feet?" Crystal tipped her head toward the man who was mowing the grass around the mailbox at the end of the driveway and rolled her eyes. "No, I can still bend that much, if I'm sitting. See?" She stretched forward and drew up one leg, touching her toes. "'Course, if I did that standing up, I'd tip over! Oh my god, I'm turning into such a cow!"

"You are not; you look cute, pregnant. Everybody says so."

"Even with these feet?"

Nearing the end of her pregnancy, with her hair and eyes shining and her face rosy, Crystal looked younger in her thirties than she had during her twenties, Margie thought. Unnoticed, she looked closely at Crystal's face as her daughter pressed at her toes, at her arch. With the creation of new life had Crystal's terrifying dreams permanently disappeared, or were they patiently awaiting the birth with the same degree of anticipation as was Margie? The shadow behind the shine of Crystal's blue-brown eyes shimmered hungrily over the faint lines that lay just below the bloom of her complexion. Margie shivered, then to disperse the shadows laughed aloud *shadows, you are so faint you are all but unseen; unseen you all but disappear* at the pleasure that Crystal took in being pregnant, the joy she shared by calling attention to her swollen feet, to her being able to polish her toenails only if she was sitting. She considered asking if Crystal and Dag had considered moving into Beryl's empty trailer, wished she lived closer by. Their apartment in Mesabi was a twenty-mile distance from Sweetgrass, and the cabin was near the far side of the reservation; still, she was not much more than a half hour away.

"So, you think it worked out, walling up the porch?" Margie leaned against the widened doorway between the front room and the sunroom that had been the porch, looking into the house. When she'd moved into management at Chi-Waabik Casino, the

Mozhay Point reservation housing authority had granted her a low-interest home improvement loan on the cabin in her name, after she'd signed to lease the cabin and the land allotment it stood on from the legal descendants of Half-dime LaForce, her own grandfather. It amused her to be her own landlord. She'd put in a furnace and a shower, got a new roof and wiring, and enclosed the front porch, with a small deck outside the door. She'd run out of money before she got to fixing up the kitchen, but bought a new stove and refrigerator on her credit card and moved the wood-stove out of the kitchen into the attached shed. She then used her income tax refund to buy a stacking washer and dryer that fit next to the kitchen sink. The house looked great, Margie knew; she wanted to hear it from Crystal.

"Well, even though I liked the way the place looked a lot better when it still had the porch, it is nice to sit in here. And with the deck right out the door, it's kind of like having the porch, anyway." Crystal's voice was breathy; she sat up straighter to give herself a little more air.

"Only better."

"Worked good; the whole place looks good. But that furnace isn't big enough; I hope you don't freeze to death in the winter." This last, ominously. Crystal hadn't wanted her mother to move back into the cabin.

Well, *we* never did, you and me. But Margie didn't say it. That was about as good as she was going to get out of Crystal, she thought. "Help me with the salad, will you? Here, come in the kitchen and peel something."

Crystal sliced cucumbers and tomatoes and peeled an avocado, sitting at the same wooden table that had been in the cabin the day Margie had met Zho Wash, and for who knew how long before that. The whole table was marked up with gouges and stains that Margie sanded lightly every few years, but she couldn't bring herself to paint over the marks made by all that living that had gone on in the cabin over the decades before she had moved in, and the decades since. The sight of those blemishes on the wood and the feel when she ran her hands over the tabletop brought to mind Zho setting a hot frying pan full of walleye on the table, or Michael's beautiful hands trimming porcupine quills with a toenail clipper under a plastic bread bag ("You want to try it? Be careful; these things can fly up and put your eye out."), or little Crystal tipping over a bowl of blueberries with maple sugar and wild rice.

Or Margie, slicing potatoes to soak in salt water, watching an ice storm coat everything with a wet shine outside the little window over the table and wondering where Zho could be, worrying that his truck would slide, skid over the ice, and that he might be hurt. That afternoon she had bitten her fingernails down, tasting starch and acid from the potatoes, until they stung with the touch of salt water. Had watched the clouds cover over the sky, the sun set, the woods around the cabin darken, while she waited. Had set the table, heated canned beans, potatoes, corn. Had worried, would the truck skid on ice; would he slide off the road and be hurt? Had worried, had worried.

When the truck had finally cantered up the driveway she had heard herself say, "It's Zho Wash," as though she were another person talking, a different Margie, and wondered what else she heard beneath the words.

"See how pretty it is outside?" he asked.

"It looks slippery. You could have gone off the road." She had helped carry groceries in with wet, sore hands and dropped a carton of eggs on the floor.

"See how pretty it is outside?" he asked again.

Kneeling, sopping up shell and runny egg with Zho, she looked down, sniffed as tears ran off the end of her nose and mixed with the eggs. She mopped them with her sweatshirt sleeve just before they stood to shake the mess from dishcloths into the garbage can, looking away in order that Zho not see her face.

"Margie-enjiss, it's all right. It's all right, Margie; come out on the porch with me, and we'll watch the storm."

The old man embraced Margie, patted her shoulder, and she took a step closer into the comfort of his soft old blue chambray shirt. Below his collarbone she found shelter, a faint hollow that had been made for the side of her head to rest in. He smelled like Tide, she thought, and tobacco; she wrapped her arms around his waist, leaning against Zho, who supported her, shifting their weight slowly from his left foot to his right, right to left, whispering, sh, sh.

"Gid akoz, ina? *Are you sick?" Zho asked. "Are you sad?"*

"I was scared."

"There's nothing out here to be frightened of. Listen, can you hear it? The ice, it sounds like it's singing. There's nothing going to hurt you in the woods."

How to explain her fear? "There's bears out there." Her head rested in the hollow of blue chambray; in the V of his open collar she could see, above the Tide whiteness of his T-shirt, his brown throat and the comet spray of pale, shiny scars where he had been shot during the Second World War. She raised and turned her head to indicate the window, where a bear might be seen if there was one and if he looked, and her lips brushed his throat, above the neckband of the T-shirt, and stayed.

Zho bent to rest his cheek against the top of her head. "They're mostly sleeping now. They're more afraid of you than you are of them."

Margie inhaled the smoky comfort that was Zho's skin, and ex-haled warm air that mixed with the scent of Zho and became part of her next breath. I'm not afraid of bears, she would have said, but instead chose to inch closer, as cautiously and subtly as she could, and then closer yet, to the source of that heady scent. In a moment she would be so close to Zho that she would cross the barrier that was his shirt, undershirt, and skin; she would look fearlessly out at the world through Zho's eyes. In a moment.

"*Margie-ens,*" *Zho Wash said, and kissed her.*

His lips were soft, closed, gentlemanly, of another generation. And as a gentleman of that generation, he was resolute.

What was she thinking? She removed her arms from around Zho's waist and crossed and wrapped them around her own, pulled out a chair, and sat at the table. "I can't do this."

He sighed, cleared his throat.

"I'm sorry."

"It's all right, Margie-enjiss. There's nothing to be sorry about."

"Really?"

"Of course not. Gi bakade na? *You hungry?* Wiisinni daa. *Come on, let's eat.*" *And he took off his boots and set them on the rag rug by the door and then put the groceries away while she reheated the beans, potatoes, and corn, keeping a considerate distance between their bodies as they moved back and forth between the cookstove and the cupboard, the table and the sink, the refrigerator and the woodbox. And ate in considerate silence, pausing as he always did to look at his place and say his unspoken prayer, commenting as he always did after the first bite,* "Mino pagwad, *tastes good,*" *and eating steadily and appreciatively. And then boiled up a saucepan of coffee on the stove and poured it into two cups, stirring sugar into both, placing on the table in front of Margie the white one with the band of pink flowers and gold rim because he knew she liked that one the best.*

She rested her folded arms on the edge of the table and leaned over the cup of coffee, a black, black jewel in a pink flowered gold setting. "I just can't," *she said lamely.* "I can't."

He looked directly at her then, and poured a little coffee from his own cup, the green one with the chip and stains, into a saucer, to cool it. He lifted the saucer and drank. "Everything is all right, Margie."

"I should leave here and go back home."

"You do what you need to do. You can do anything you want to do." *He said it kindly, though his even, old man's voice was sounding somewhat husky.*

"But I can't do that. You know."

"I would never try to make you do anything you didn't want to do."

"You wouldn't?"

"No, I never would."

And that was the reason that Margie sanded the battered old wooden table only every couple of years, and then very lightly, and never covered the peachskin softness of the wood with varnish or paint. Because she loved the blemishes and their memories so, in middle age she protected them by covering the table when she worked with a flowered plastic tablecloth, to keep them intact.

She took her apron from the hook by the sink and tied the strings in back at the waist, dug a bowl and wooden spoon, flour and baking powder from the cupboard, and began measuring, two hands of flour, small palm of baking powder, little bit of sugar, half a pinch of salt. "I'm making just a half a batch."

"Frybread!" Crystal's voice was pleasure and dismay, her pursed mouth a cluster of birdberries that a lip-reader would have interpreted as disapproval on the first syllable and a kiss on the second. Margie felt pale, old, and happy enough to weep in the presence of her ripeness. "I can only eat a little piece! I'm not even hungry, anyway."

"Want me to open that window?" Margie asked. Crystal had told her that the smell of frying made her stomach turn lately.

"I'll get it. Don't make much; Animoosh doesn't need to eat that either."

"I'm mixing just a half a batch." Margie didn't suggest that if she made a full batch, Crystal could take leftover frybread home. Once her bread left the allotment it seemed to lose some of its magic; if he got hungry for it the next day perhaps Dag would drive her little girl back to Sweetgrass for another visit.

For Crystal's sake supper was light, just salad and frybread and iced raspberry tea, in consideration of her wayward, and Margie hoped temporary, tiny appetite. Dag, after finishing the frybread, sighed, a hungry man. "Any more?" he asked hopefully.

"I can mix some more up in . . .

(dirty look from Crystal)

. . . want some hardboiled eggs? There's some in a bowl in the fridge," Margie answered. "You can have them all." He ate three and left two for his mother-in-law.

When it was time for Margie to get ready for her shift at the casino, Dag walked his wife to the car with his hand on the small of her back, opened the door for her, and helped her into her seat. He treated her so deferentially, Margie thought, so aware of the new life she carried, the sacredness of new life that would take the place of someone else's before very long. *Whose place will this little one take*, she wondered; at the thought of the shadows stirring behind the blue-brown shine of Crystal's eyes, she shivered again.

"Well, call me if you have that baby," she said. "Don't forget!" *I pray for your safety, Nindaaniss, for your happiness.*

Dag laughed. "I'll call you before we even go the hospital! Somebody has to help me keep her in line!" His arm around Margie's shoulders, he bent to look directly into her face, as was his way. Dag's light hazel eyes were understanding, his smile hopeful and encouraging.

He was so cute, Margie thought, with those red cheeks, like he was blushing, and that dark blond crewcut. She reached into the car to stroke her daughter's hair, soft and fine as a child's. What a shame that she wore it almost as short as her husband's, but Margie wasn't going to say a word. Crystal had cut it when she had started LPN training.

"I know what you're thinking; don't say it. I like it this way; it's easier to take care of, and it's out of my way at the clinic. So don't say anything."

"I was just looking at the color. I think your baby might have red hair! That can happen, you know, when a person with dark hair marries somebody who's blond."

Crystal rolled her eyes at Dag, who laughed and waved as he started the car. "See you later, Margie! Don't work too hard! Thanks for the supper!"

Margie walked with the car as it backed down the driveway, and stood at the side of the road, waving, until Crystal and Dag were out of sight.

As they drove down the road away from Sweetgrass and out of the reservation, Dag said, "She seems lonely."

"No wonder, living out in the middle of the woods by herself like that. Nobody next door since Sis passed and Beryl moved out of the trailer. You would think the quiet would get to her."

"She could use more company. Be nice if somebody moved into the trailer."

"What she could use is a boyfriend." Crystal made a pfft sound. "That'll be the day!"

"Your mom's nice-looking, a good-looking woman. She could meet somebody, if she wanted to. She's still young."

"She wouldn't be able to handle it. She's stuck in the past; she'll never move on and she'll never move. Why do you think she went through all that mess to lease her family's old allotment? And now she's all by herself in that house. Staying on that place. Gawd. So stubborn."

"You may be right; who would ever want a stubborn woman like that?" asked Dag. "I'd never have one!" Crystal looked over at him suspiciously. "I don't even know any women like that, do you?" Crystal snorted; they both laughed.

"When we get home, you want to go to the Dairy Queen?" asked Crystal. She felt an appetite coming back, as well as the need for a cigarette. After they got back to the apartment, maybe she would get one from the stash she kept in her underwear drawer, wrapped and hidden in a pair of long johns, and go for a walk by herself.

~ ~ ~

When Margie pulled into her space in the employees' section of the Chi Waabik Casino in the Woods parking lot to start her shift, the guest lot was nearly full, and cars were starting to park out at the side of the road. In the marble-tiled entryway to the restaurant, Enchanted Agwaching, a line of people leaned against the wall of windows that looked out over Lost Lake, waiting for their silent pagers to light and vibrate, welcoming them inside the restaurant for "traditional Native dinners, elegantly served in the enchantment of our comfortable indoor forest." At $19.95 for a walleye and wild rice supper, people should expect a lot of comfort and elegance, she thought, not to mention a pretty big plateful of enchanting food.

In the women's dressing room she changed into her Guest Services uniform and SAS shoes with the arch inserts, and twisted her ponytail into a knot that she secured to the back of her head with a beaded barrette. She hung her street clothes and purse in her locker and checked her appearance in the full-length mirror, under the sign that read, "You only get ONE chance to make a first impression!" Looking back to check her out was a middle-aged woman with heavy bangs that curved above her glasses, in Margie's concierge outfit of white shirt, black stretch pants, black shoes, and black satin bow tie. The bib of her blouse had rows of tucks running down the front and was starched to the consistency of paper. Her red sleeve garters and name tag were trimmed with red and blue beads in a geometric design. Her quilled earrings matched the colors of the flowers beaded onto her barrette.

She had gotten busty over the years, and thick around the middle, thought Margie, turning to the side and pressing in her stomach with one hand. She unbuckled her red cummerbund in the back and loosened the front, covering her curvy paunch. Better. She pulled on her black tuxedo jacket as she entered Guest Services through the back door, pinning her name tag (Margie Robineau: Your Chi Waabik Casino in the Woods Concierge) over her heart.

"I'm here, Bubba," she told the first-shift concierge. "You ready to go?"

" 's all yours, Margie. You're early! Vicky's in the upstairs ladies' bathroom; somebody up there was feeling like she was going to faint. Jerry's over by the west-side slots. June went to the gift shop to get some more promo bags; she'll be right back to help Les at the counter. No problems today; we had to call Security about an hour ago because some guy got mad over at the blackjack tables. What else . . . oh, phone rang a lot, not for you; I'd have said so in the first place. Anyway, I'm out of here. Maybe I'll see you later; my dad was saying he wanted to play bingo tonight. Don't forget to take your supper break."

"Wait, wait a second. Where's Andi?"

"Oh, she just went over to the motel side. One of the guests left her purse in the bingo hall. She'll be back. I haven't seen her yet, myself, so good luck!" Bubba opened the safe combination in seconds, replaced his master key and handed Margie hers, slammed the safe shut. "Gotta run!" The reservation business director had told Margie and Bubba that the next time that Andi showed up at work with that dirty mess of a hairdo, whoever was on duty was going to have to tell her to clean herself up.

"See you!" Bubba could move very quickly, for such a heavy man.

She was paged ten minutes into her shift, and nearly ran to the desk.

"It's the Mesabi hospital," June whispered. "Just leave; we'll cover for you." Everyone knew about Margie's grandchild. "Take the loon under Jack and Dale Ann."

The house telephones had been custom-made for Chi Waabik's Enchanted Forest theme in the shape of loons frozen into iridescent blue plastic bases that reflected the casino's fluorescent lighting to imitate the sundance on Lost Lake. On their backs were number pads; their red glass eyes glowed when the phones were in use, blinked when the caller was on hold. The Mozhay Pointers had nicknamed them "the loon-a-phones." The one that Margie picked up was on a surprisingly lifelike resin birch-bark table. On the pine-paneled wall above hung a large, gilt-framed portrait of a Mozhay Point couple. The man wore a floral-beaded black velvet vest over a white shirt and red tie. His smile was open and welcoming (we are so glad to see you and your money, our special guests), his eyeglasses framed in banker-gray plastic and straight on his face (but we will put up with no nonsense; don't try to fool with the Indians). The woman rested both hands, fingers laced, on his arm. Her fingernails were long, French-manicured; on her left hand was a thin-banded engagement ring set with a tiny stone; on her right a large marquise diamond flanked by sapphires. The dark periwinkle blue of her sweater complemented the silver-and-pepper of her fluffy hair; her kind eyes and lips smiled reservedly but pleasantly, as was appropriate for the wife of an elected tribal official. "Welcome and Warm Greetings from the Mozhay Point Band of Ojibwe Tribal Chairman Jack Minogeezhik and Mrs. Dale Ann Minogeezhik," the brass plate at the bottom of the portrait captioned.

As she always did when she passed the portrait, Margie wondered momentarily and subconsciously at Dale Ann's metamorphosis from frumpy to stylish, from dumpy to trim. And as she always did, she avoided looking at the framed photographs on the opposite wall, where a more resolute Jack was flanked by the four elected Mozhay Point tribal council representatives: Archie DuCharme, Doreen Rice Bird, Michael Washington, and Tammy Simon. With her unusually good peripheral vision, however, her eyes focused immediately and unwillingly on Michael's photo, which photoflashed onto her retina as it did every time.

The phone winked at her. "What do you know, old loon?" Margie asked. She mouthed "migwech" to June, lifted the loon's back from its body, and spoke into the part of the receiver that on a real loon would have rested just above the heart. "Hello? This is Margie." She was a little short of breath.

Before she left Chi Waabik she called Theresa's house and then Merrilee's, leaving messages for Michael at both.

~ ~ ~

At the hospital she drove around the back and parked in her usual spot close to the nursing home entrance. The ward clerk waved as she passed the desk. "Hello, Margie; he's resting right now." Margie turned into the hallway to the Convalescent Care ward.

There was a rerun of *The Brady Bunch* on the television in Zho Wash's room. Crystal was watching from the recliner next to the old man's bed, curled around her stomach, and snorting over Marcia's dilemma over who to go to the dance with. "Suck it up, Princess," she muttered. She had put sweatpants on under her red maternity dress, changed her sandals for tennies and socks, and was wearing one of Dag's jackets. Maybe the baby would be a little girl who looked like Crystal, Margie thought.

"He's been asleep since I got here; nobody's been by," Crystal said.

He looked all right, Margie thought, kissing him lightly on the top of his head, but so frail under that big pile of blankets. She looked through the small stack of pictures on the bedside table: one each of Eva and Lucy, Crystal, Margie herself, Michael and Theresa, and their four children and six grandchildren.

A woman who looked familiar to Margie took a clipboard from its hook on the outside of the door and entered the room. She spoke quietly, in a pitch just below the television, each of her sentences a question. "Um, Mrs. Robineau, I'm Angie Maki? I'm usually over at the Miskwaa clinic? But I'll be Mr. Washington's nurse tonight, and I'm the chaplain on call, too? Has anyone talked with you about Mr. Washington's situation?"

"He didn't eat today and has been sleeping most of the time is what they told me when they called." Where did she know her from?

"The daytime staff said he was a little lethargic this morning and didn't want much of his breakfast? Then he refused any lunch. They brought him to the atrium this afternoon because he usually likes to look at the birds and tried to feed him some Jell-O? But he didn't want to swallow. On the way back to his room the aide said she thought he fainted in the wheelchair? He has been asleep off and on since that time."

"He hasn't eaten much at all for quite a while; he's been going downhill." Margie took a deep breath, blinked, wiped her nose with a tissue from the box on the bedside table. Zho was so still. *Nibaa ina*, she asked silently, and placed a hand on his chest; it moved. Ah. He was breathing. "Do you think he knows we're here?"

"I think they do, Mrs. Robineau; Mr. Washington might be hearing us right now while he rests; I think their spirits know ours even when the body might not show it." Margie and the woman watched Zho's face as Margie stroked his chest. "Mrs. Robineau, do you remember me, Angelique Dommage? I used to babysit Crystal sometimes, when she was little, and I worked at bingo, too? I stayed at Earl and Alice's, down the road? Alice was my auntie."

Of course, it was Angelique. She had filled out and permed her hair. Little Angie! "Yes, I remember you. Crystal, you remember Angie. It has been a long time. What did you say your name is now?"

"It's Maki. I've been living in the Cities, and we just moved to Mesabi for my husband's job? And I work part-time at the Miskwaa clinic and just started fill-ins here, too? I'm on all night, so I'll be somewhere around the hospital if you need anything. Just ask at the nurse's station, and they'll page me."

"What did she say she is? A nun?" Aunt Beryl was pulling back and forth at the railing that lined the hallways, trying to turn and maneuver her wheelchair into the room.

Zho Wash heard the women talking, and had been listening to Marcia Brady's problems, too, but there was another reality going on back of his eyelids, and he had no desire to lift them or to allow Beryl the opportunity to try to draw him into a one-sided conversation. Ever since Sis died it seemed that Beryl commemorated their close friendship by combining both of their personalities, one sweet and one spicy, into a single existence, which was a little more than what he could take in these days.

"Boonitoon, daga; leave it alone, my dear," she directed Angie, who had grasped the handles on the back of the chair and was pushing it as Beryl pulled, and pulling as Beryl pushed. "I can do that; how about you go down to my room and get my slippers, would you, those big pink gripper socks on the floor by my bed."

Crystal opened her eyes and stretched, her hands crossed above and in back of her head. "Hi, Auntie Beryl. What do you want, your socks? Want me to get them?"

"I'll do it, Crystal; you stay here and visit with your auntie." Angie neatly finessed the wheelchair into the room and left.

"How's your father doing?" Beryl asked.

"That bum? He hasn't shown up here yet."

Beryl looked hard at Margie, who bent to tuck the corners of the blankets into the bottom of the bed. "This place is a mess," she commented.

"You know who that was, don't you? That was Angelique Dommage. That girl, what has she done to herself?" Beryl said. "Looks sort of like a man with that haircut."

And how many years had Beryl been wearing that teased-up beehive hairdo, thought Margie, all permanented and colored and hairsprayed, looking sort of like a football player in a blue-black helmet herself. "On some women, short hair looks good," she said, delicately pointing her chin toward her daughter.

"Crystal, she always looks cute; every hairdo suits her," decreed the Elder. "And she'll grow it out when she gets tired of it, anyway; won't you, little Mother?"

"Crystal." Unheard, Zho Wash spoke her name as he opened his eyes to see her, young and carrying a new life, her head held high on her long neck, her hair short and crisp-looking. When she was born she had struggled to free herself on her own from her mother's body; her hands, crossed and bound back of her head by the umbilical cord, were the first part of her that he saw. Margie's belly had moved and heaved as the baby pushed the rest of her body out with her feet. The cord was wound around her wrists; she kicked and struggled until he loosened the cord to free them, then calmly looked him and Margie over with those muddy, blue-brown eyes.

Remember what a skinny baby she had been? What was that he had called her, to tease Margie?

"Hey, Chicken Legs," he tried to say. He was surprised that he could hardly move his lips; his words came out as a creaky sigh.

"Hi, Grandpa Zho," she answered.

He looked at her stomach, his lips moved to form the word, "baby."

Crystal nodded. "Any day, now. Maybe tomorrow, maybe next week."

"Abinoojii kwii-wii-sens? Baby boy?"

"Maagizhaa. Amanj i dash."

The old man closed his eyes, wishing that she would continue, the little sweetheart, talking Indian in her funny voice.

"Is he asleep?" asked Beryl. "Crystal, why don't you take me back to my room? We haven't had a good visit in a long time."

Margie raised her eyebrows.

"You take care of Zho Wash, Margie; he needs you." It was long past time, after all, for Crystal to understand things.

~ ~ ~

A few days after Crystal was born, the visiting nurse from the county had come to the cabin. Beryl was there, ready to take on anybody from the government who tried to talk another unwed Indian girl into giving her baby up for adoption. She had straightened up the cabin, washed the floors, shined everything up for the nurse's report, and stood right there by the bed as the nurse weighed and measured the baby and counted her parts. She helped Margie answer questions as the nurse filled out the birth certificate, prepared to order the nurse from the cabin if things came to that.

"Your name?"

"Margaret Mary Robineau."

"Age?"

"Twenty-one."

"Permanent residence?"

"With me," Beryl answered. "Route 1, box 4, Sweetgrass Township."

"The father's name?"

Zho spoke from the chair next to the woodstove. "Joseph Washington," he said firmly. Beryl's eyebrows raised; white ringed the dark gray-brown irises of her eyes. Her mouth opened, and closed.

The nurse thought Zho had misunderstood. She asked, "We need to know who the baby's father is. Whose baby is she?"

Zho answered, "Mine. She's my baby. I'm the father."

The nurse clicked her tongue, shame on you, and wrote "Joseph Washington" on the birth certificate. Zho and Margie signed at the bottom. Thanking the nurse for all of her trouble and encouraging her to leave, Beryl and Zho walked her out to her car and watched her drive away; then Beryl said, "That's your baby? It is not."

"Yes, she is; isn't that my name on the birth certificate?"

"You're not going to make Michael take any responsibility for that poor girl; you're going to support this baby? When will this ever end? He's just like his mother, and you'll never change."

"I'm the father," Zho repeated.

Beryl shut her mouth for poor Margie's sake and went back to the cabin every day for the next week or so to help with the cooking and cleaning, to keep Margie's spirits up with a magazine, a flower in a vase. To make sure her milk was in and flowing, that the baby was eating and digesting. Poor Margie, abandoned like that, with no place to go to and nobody but that old man and Beryl to take care of her. Michael was who knew where; last Beryl had heard he was in Minneapolis, living off that Theresa and his mother. Margie, she must have been heartbroken and mortified to have to ask Michael's father to take her in, yet she put up a good front, even seemed happy, sitting in the rocking chair nursing her baby. Well, that was what falling in love with a baby could do, thought Beryl. It was clear to see what that tiny girl meant to her, and Zho did treat them both like they were his own, which she supposed they were; after all, Michael had fathered Margie's baby (or hadn't he?), and that was Zho's grandchild (wasn't that so?). And with the baby coming so quickly that it was born right there in the cabin, with only Zho to help, well, between that and his son's being the father (wasn't that right?), she could see how he would want to take care of the child and her mother. He had lost his first wife, had never divorced Lucy, had given her most of everything he had for Michael, had lived alone for much of his life.

"They'll be good for each other, can help each other out, Zho and Margie," Beryl said aloud to herself, and decided to not think further about the baby girl's parentage, for the time being. Out loud, anyway.

~ ~ ~

These days, younger people often raise their voices when they speak to me. "Auntie Beryl!" or "Mrs. Dublebon!" they nearly shout, thinking that I am either hard of hearing or sliding off into dementia. The truth is, I will answer their questions about warm milk or if I need to use the toilet when I am ready to do so.

What I am giving a great deal of thought to these days is the past. A great deal of it is painful, our past, but nevertheless it is ours and has its beautiful aspects that outweigh the pain. We take the bad with the good, and acknowledge this to the Great Spirit who is also God in our morning prayer, giving thanks that we were born Anishinaabe.

But you can't help the way you feel. These days I also feel crabby, and it's no wonder that I do. My body has weakened and failed considerably; here in Convalescent Care there is no opportunity to rice, to maple sugar, or to chop wood. That, combined with my age, of course, has led to this: I no longer have that impressive upper-body strength that Anishinaabe women are famous for. My arms can still move the wheelchair, if I take it slow, but right now Crystal is pushing me down the hall to my room, which is all right because it gives me some time to think.

What shall I tell this young woman, whose eyes tell to the world the story of the Anishinaabe people? How we were redeemed through the sacrifice of Muskrat's life is recounted in the very color of Crystal's eyes, the blue of water and the brown of earth that, to one who looks more closely, emphasizes the clarity of the shadows behind the surface; the past is always with us, and Crystal will carry it into the future when she brings new life into our world. The old Anishinaabeg, the ancestors whose shadows began to awaken once she passed childhood, stir occasionally as they wait for the time that she will begin to understand and to speak. *Crystal will tell of our past; that is her destiny, determined by God the Creator, who in giving her life set her path, uncertain though it has sometimes appeared, in this direction. Before she can do that, she will need to gather the strength that will come from knowing her own story.*

What shall I say to this young woman, whose round belly full of life held and cradled by her hips gently bumps the back of my head from time to time as she wheels her weakened and failing old auntie down the hall of Convalescent Care? She turns the wheelchair smoothly through the doorway, just as she is being taught in her nursing classes: no herky-jerky, and a nice snaking around to the side of my bed.

My roommate, Dorothy, looks like something from a wax museum, all swaddled up tightly in a white cotton thermal blanket. Her hands, folded on her chest, twine in her fingers a rosary so long it looks like it has no end, with large oval beads green as emeralds. Hearing the wheelchair, she opens her eyes. "Have they found him, Mother?" she asks.

"Not yet; I'll wake you up when they do. Go back to sleep," I answer.

"All right, Mother," the swaddled daughter answers, and closes her eyes.

I roll myself to the bedside table and turn on a small desk lamp. "Sit awhile, Crystal," I invite, and point with my chin. "If you open my closet drawer, you'll see a bag of butter mints. Bring them over here, why don't you?"

Crystal reverses the tight twist that I had put into the plastic bag to keep things fresh and offers them to me.

"Try one yourself first, would you, to see how fresh they are?" I ask, gathering more closely some of the story's more unruly vines and tendrils. "I try to be careful not to crack my plate."

Chewing a yellow butter mint that was soft enough to not crack my plate, Crystal signals with a thumbs-up, and I begin to speak.

~ ~ ~

Zho Wash felt warm fingers on the side of his neck, on that smooth and poreless spray of pale pink scars, resting lightly to feel his pulse, and realized that he had been sleeping, that the room had been quiet and dark for some time. He heard her breathing softly as she rolled the table away from the bed, slowly, so as to not awaken him. Margie, he thought. Young, she had traced the trail with soft young fingers in the dark, where its silvery pink reflected the moon, he remembered. It made her think of the trail of a shooting star, she had said. Margie-ens, he thought, and again opened his eyes.

He could see her by the half-light from the hallway, dressed in the mannish work getup she wore to the casino. The outfit amused him: it didn't suit her figure at all, did nothing for the curves she had developed over the years. She bent to look into his face, tilting her head back slightly because of her bifocals. The little scooped-out half-moons on the bottom of her glasses amused him too, and the white streaks in the hair she pulled back from her temples into that ponytail, for work. Margie, disguised as the big chief *ogema* boss lady, the middle-aged, no-baloney Chi Waabik concierge.

"Little mother," he said. "Boozhoo *aneen*."

"You're awake."

"*Gi wi-nibaa, ina?* You tired?"

"*Eya, bun-gee*; just a little bit."

He watched her, the mother of his little girl, prepare for bed. She unclipped the barrette from the back of her head, pulled the elastic band from her ponytail, ruffled her loosened hair, and shook it. Her glasses, watch, and earrings she laid on the bedside table that she had rolled to the window, with the barrette and band. She writhed out of her black tuxedo jacket, shook it, and hung it over the back of the chair; unbuckled (with a sigh and a deep breath) and folded her red cummerbund on top of the jacket. From the top drawer in the built-in locker she pulled a pair of men's cotton pajamas that she unfolded, sniffing for the scent of the bar of Yardley lavender soap that she kept in each drawer. Modestly she pulled the pajama shirt on over her shoulders and removed her white blouse; thus covered, she finished changing. She hung the blouse on the hook behind the bathroom door on top of a blue-striped cotton bathrobe, and folded her slacks over the cummerbund. She walked soundlessly to the window, where she opened the drapes to the moon and stars. At the side of the bed she bent to lay a hand on the old man's chest, between the buttons of his pajama top, to stroke the skin that felt thin and cool, unable to hold in heat. Bending close and closer until their faces almost touched she saw that his eyes looked young and trusting. She lifted the blankets and carefully fit her body close to Zho Wash's, on her side, turned toward him. She draped one arm above the pillow, the other across Zho's chest, and lay with the side of her head braced on her upper arm and her nose and lips against the top of his head. He tugged the strand of her hair that lay across his chest, twisting it gently to watch its silver-white filaments pull, reflect, and hold the fluorescent light from the hallway and the blue light from the moon, and held it in the hand that rested against her breast.

"Margie-enjiss," he whispered, and fell asleep.

~ ~ ~

In early morning not long before the sun rose, Crystal dimmed the hallway lights before opening the door to Zho Wash's room. Fingers laced across the top of her stomach, she stood in the doorway as her father's eyes opened.

The Occasional Scent of Sweetgrass

2008

FOR THE PAST TWENTY MINUTES OR SO I have heard the sounds of the Mesabi Convalescent Care night shift getting ready to hand us, elders grown fragile in body, mind, or both, to the next day. Those of us to whom the Creator has given this day, I should say, since every week or so the day begins with the soft sounds (shuffles, faint thumps, murmurs of the nursing home staff, the roll of gurney wheels that sounds like bowling) of one of us being carefully handed over to the van driver from the Mesabi Mortuary.

Today might be your turn, Zho Wash. I say this to myself without speaking; my voice, an aged man's husky squeak, is unreliable. It comes and goes, but mostly goes, these days.

Through the crack where the drawn drapes don't quite meet, I have been watching as the blackness of a starless night sky has faded to the dark and dusty color of blueberries. *Miinan geezhig*, I think, *blueberry sky*. At the workstation down the hall, the nurse is rattling papers and speaking to the ward clerk in a shift boss voice, like the voice my own little Margie-ens, who is asleep alongside me in the hospital bed with her sweet face just inches from mine, uses in her job at the reservation casino where she is the boss of the four-to-midnight evening shift. I hear the ward clerk tapping those no-nonsense words from the nurse onto the keyboard like a tired, nervous pigeon while she thinks about her husband at home in their warm bed. I can hear what's on her mind: *He's getting up about now*, she thinks as her fingers jitter notes about the residents' nights onto the computer screen. *If I can leave this place right at seven, and if he gets the kids ready for school on time so that they don't miss the bus, the bed might still be warm when I get under the covers.*

This could be the day, I think. I can smell that the orderly has put on the coffee for the day shift: he makes it early in order to allow it to stew into that thickness that they like. In a few minutes it will have that nice, bitter burning scent that lures Margie from sleep. She has been, as she always is when she stays in my room, careful to stay on the edge of the hospital bed, on her side and turned toward me. She sleeps with one arm across my chest and the other above the pillow, the side of her head braced on her bicep and her nose and lips against the top of my head. The smell of the coffee will work its magic into Margie's early-morning dreams, waking her. Carefully then she will roll from the bed to her feet; softly, so as not to wake me, she will walk barefoot into the little hospital bathroom to wash and dress, her feet brushing the tile floor sounding like the night breeze stirring the branches of the tamaracks at home. The question *will this be the day?* will nag at her the while. After she has washed and dressed, she will stand by the bed to watch me and place a hand under the blanket, on my chest, to feel and reassure herself that I live, anxious at first because my breathing has become so light and difficult to hear over the noises of the nursing home. At the weight of her hand I will inhale and exhale as deeply as I can, and my chest will rise, but only slightly; I am a very old man, much older than Margie-enjiss. She will feel, and then see, her hand move. Ah, she will think in relief, and kiss me, and leave for our house over at the LaForce allotment where she will wait for our daughter, Crystal, to call.

The land allotment on the reservation belongs to Margie's

family and is called by everyone, myself included, the LaForce Allotment, although it was once the home of my family, the Wazhushkag, the Muskrats who through *jiibik ozhibii-igewin,* the magic writing of the Indian agent's pen, in ink blacker than the orderly's coffee, became the Washingtons. Because it is only nearly dawn, and the night shift is only preparing to leave, and Margie is not yet awake, there is time for me to recount the story of how those things came to be.

～ ～ ～

Mewinzhaa, a long time ago

It was more than a hundred years ago, when my father Wazhushk, who would become Joseph Muskrat, was a boy, that the Mozhay Point Indian Reservation was cut in half and the people of the Miskwaa Rapids Band of Chippewa Indians lost the Miskwaa River as well as all of the land within three hundred feet of the riverbanks. The land west of the river was ceded to the State of Minnesota, and the Indians who had been living there were directed to move to the remaining eastern half of the reservation, which was then divided up into allotments, forty-acre pieces of property that were assigned to individual members of the band. Anything left, all land that was not assigned to individual allotment holders, was held in trust for future allotting or sale, as was the money the Miskwaa Rapids Band was promised in return for reluctantly ceding away most of its homeland.

The federal Indian agent, that was Mr. Oliver in those days, told my grandfather Little Muskrat that because the Muskrat family was not listed on the 1854 treaty as part of the Miskwaa Rapids Band, the land they lived on in the eastern half of Mozhay Point had been allotted to another family. The small board house that Little Muskrat had built and the seasonal camps that had given them subsistence would no longer be theirs to occupy but would become the property of the LaForce family, who because they were listed on the treaty as Miskwaa Rapids Band members would leave the west side of Mozhay, leave their camps, their house, and the profitable living they had been making on the west side of the river by trading pelts and buying and selling household goods and sundries.

As a boy my father was called Wazhushk, Muskrat, as were the men of the generations before him: his father Waazhkens, Little Muskrat; his grandfather Chi Wazhushk, Big Muskrat; his great-grandfather also Wazhushk. At the St. Francis Mission School that was not far from the LaForce allotment on the dirt road turnoff later called the Dionne Fork, he was baptized and given a new name, Joseph. When Mr. Oliver filled out the first year's census papers, he recorded the family's names in *Shaaganaashiimowin*, English, as Joe Muskrat Sr.; his wife, Martha Ozhawaa'ikwe Muskrat; and son, Joseph Muskrat. The agent thought that Muskrat was a humorous name, not knowing anything about the courage and sacrifice of Wazhushk during the days of the Great Flood, when water covered the entire earth.

"Where did you get that name Muskrat, Joseph?" he had asked Wazhushk the next year as he filled out another census form. "I can change it right now, to Milton, or McDaniel. Tell your father that I can do that."

"Wegonen? What did he say?" asked Little Muskrat.

"He cannot help it that he is ignorant; be respectful," Ozhawaa'ikwe said quietly, her head down, her voice directed toward her lap, her eyes on the moccasin she was turning inside out. She was ignored by Mr. Oliver, whose Ojibwe vocabulary didn't include those adjectives.

"What do you say, Joseph?"

"Thank you, no," the boy answered, politely.

Washington, wrote the agent.

Because Wazhushk had been to the school and knew English very well, he had to help translate between Mr. Oliver and his father, Little Muskrat, who understood some *Shaaganaashiimowin*, English, words but sometimes had difficulty accepting some of the concepts. This was one of those times.

"Wazhushk, my son, tell him that I don't understand this. Don't the LaForces always do their maple sugaring at the western edge of the reservation, on the other side of the rapids, half a day's north of the hill? Why would they want to come all this way to maple sugar when they have been going to the same stand for such a long time? The woods are thick and the trees healthy and the sap pure and delightfully sweet over there. Why would they want to travel all the way over here to do that, when the maple sugaring camp they go to now is so close to their fishing and hunting camps on the other side of the rapids? Why would they wish to leave their trading post, where they have prospered so in money and luxuries?" This question from Little Muskrat was rhetorical, his way of presenting a reasonable argument.

My grandmother, Ozhawaa'ikwe, who stood a foot or so behind Wazhushk and who spoke no English at all, looked anxiously from back of his shoulder. She nodded shyly, insistently, and was ignored by the agent.

"I can't follow what he is saying," Mr. Oliver answered. "Tell him that I will explain again. All of the land west of the Miskwaa River has been ceded to the government by the Indians of the Miskwaa Rapids Band, and each family that belongs to the Miskwaa Rapids Band, whose ancestors signed the 1854 land cession treaty, has been assigned an allotment of land on the Mozhay Point Indian Reservation, which is now entirely east of the river. The LaForce family has to leave where they have been living over there west of the river, leave their trading post, and they have been given an allotment assignment over here, near Lost Lake.

The Muskrat family is going to have to leave that property. It belongs to the LaForce family now. It is their legal property, their property that has been allotted to them by the U.S. government."

My father, the boy Wazhushk who had become also Joseph Washington, told me each time that he recounted the story that Little Muskrat knew about the allotments but could not understand how it could be right that the maple sugar tree stand that our family had made camp in every spring, and all of the land that had provided for the Muskrat family since before his own father, Big Muskrat, had been born, had become a part of the LaForce allotment.

"What does this mean?" Little Muskrat asked. "Where are we supposed to go? Does he want us to trade places with the LaForce family? They are most welcome to share the camps, if they should need to be here with us."

Oliver decided to speak through the boy. "Joseph, you must remind your father, once more, that the Muskrats never signed the 1854 treaty. The Muskrats have never been a part of the Miskwaa Rapids Band. You are what the government calls 'unallotted Indians'; you have no right to the property or any allotment of land, and you must move. Your father knows this already." The agent was losing his patience.

"Where will we go?" the boy asked.

"The Muskrats will move to the east bank of the Miskwaa River, which has not been allotted to anyone. You will be free to live there along the banks, at any spot you choose, as long as you are within three hundred feet of the shore. Because that area is not going to be used at this time, as agent I have the authority to allow you to reside there until the state has a need for it."

"What will happen to us then?" this from the boy.

"Then you will have to move to another location. That could be a hundred years from now; it could be never."

"Aandakii." Little Muskrat had understood the agent's words.

"We will be aandakii, living elsewhere." He paused. I suppose it took a great deal for him to say the next, which was a capitulation and admission of defeat, a betrayal of sorts, of the stand my great-grandfather Big Muskrat had taken when the 1854 treaty was being negotiated between the clan leaders and the U.S. government. "Mr. Oliver, because we must do this now, the Muskrats will sign the treaty."

Mr. Oliver clicked his tongue, sighed. "You cannot do that, Mr. Muskrat; you know that."

"Wazhushk, remind the agent that the Chi-Shaaganaashig, the leaders of the whites, wrote this down in words on government papers: the treaty is for as long as the Miskwaa River roars over the rocks of the big rapids. Tell him, my son, that you and I are the only Muskrats who remain. Remind him that everyone else has left, or has died. I will sign the treaty on behalf of the last of us." This was spoken with his chin held high: Little Muskrat kept his dignity as he addressed this visitor graciously but firmly.

Before translating, Wazhushk, who like his father and grandfather had been named after the courageous animal hero, squared his shoulders and mimicked his father's stance, his chin high; he inhaled a great breath of cool air to settle the tears that threatened to rise to his eyes and spill.

"That doesn't matter." Mr. Oliver interrupted before the boy even spoke one word. "You know, and I know, that the Muskrats were never a part of the Miskwaa Rapids clans. Big Muskrat and his family wandered here from up north somewhere, probably Canada."

"Aandakii," the boy said under his breath. Elsewhere. The Muskrats had come from elsewhere; we were unallotted Indians who would again live elsewhere.

"He was not born in this area; neither were any of his relatives. He couldn't have signed the treaty if he had wanted to. Joseph, remind your father of that."

Little Muskrat waved his hand to say, no need to do that. "O'o dash?" he asked softly, indicating the board house that he had nailed together with lumber given out by the agent at annuity time.

Ozhawaa'ikwe, understanding, looked the agent fully in the face, which was unusual given her extreme shyness. "O'o dash?" she echoed.

"You can take anything that you would like, Mr. Muskrat, anything you can carry away; Mrs. Muskrat, you, too. The federal government is going to build another house here for the LaForce family, and I can promise you that the same will be done for you at the place you decide on by the river. I have the authority to do that. These will be warm, tar-papered lumber houses, very fine houses, with raised floors. Your missus will like that."

"Wazhushk, tell Mr. Oliver that we will think about this." Little Muskrat was a proud man.

That is how my father, and his mother and father, came to leave the place where their family had lived for some time and that had become their home. They packed their household goods that they would carry on foot to the riverbank and cleaned the board house and the yard around it of that waste that accumulates at every place that people live, in spite of their best efforts. Little Muskrat dug a pit for that, bits of birch bark and hide, discarded soup bones gnawed by raccoons, the wet mess of wood chips around the chopping block, the cracked frame for stretching hides that Ozhawaa'ikwe was saving for firewood.

Looking around the yard, Wazhushk pictured Half-dime La-Force carrying a canvas bundle bulging with worldly goods up the footpath from the trail. *Because of the trading business that he had carried on with the white homesteaders and the fur trappers, the LaForce family had many fine household conveniences; the women of the family were adorned with the pretties that awaited trade. Half-dime would have to portage ten large sacks, at least, carrying two at a time on his back to the Muskrat house, to be opened and unpacked by his mother and wife and their two little girls, who would accompany him on the last portage. Artense LaForce would be the first into the board house, holding little Henen's hand, in her other arm carrying a bundle of sprigged calico, with hanks of thread and papers of needles and pins tucked in its folds; and a rug that she had braided out of old wool blankets and shirts. Wazhushk imagined her ducking her head to enter, her silver hoop earrings absorbing and reflecting the little daylight that came in through the open doorway, commenting to her mother-in-law on the darkness inside, the smallness, her reluctance to spread the rug on the swept dirt floor. Half-dime's mother Therese followed, sucking on her clay pipe and carrying the baby, Maggie. The old woman, who dressed in the finery of her girlhood, peered into the house before entering, commented on the smoothness of the swept floor, the absence of leaves and pebbles. She shifted the baby to one hip in order to free one hand that smoothed her dress, stroking the bands of satin ribbon trim on the chest and hem that looked like rainbows against the black wool, then removed her moccasins and stepped daintily onto the rug, flexing her small feet and her tiny ankles that were bound tightly in ribbon-striped wool leggings that matched her dress. Well, Shi-gaagoons, she said (addressing her daughter-in-law by the childhood name that she knew the woman disliked), this will look pretty with all of your nice things in it. She dug in the velvet bag that she wore tied to her waist to find her own grandmother's silver crucifix, which she hung on the wall opposite the door, on the nail from which Ozhawaa'ikwe had removed her bundle of drying medicine plants. The crucifix stole the light from Artense's earrings; whatever expression was on her face was shadowed, but Wazhushk imagined distaste and discontent with Muskrat house.*

"Those LaForces," Wazhushk said as he kicked wood chips toward the pit. "Who do they think they are?"

"Not their fault, my son. They have to move, too, and leave behind that trading business they have with the trappers who come down on their way to Odanang. Not their fault. We wish them good things."

"And I will show you a secret, too, Wazhushk." Ozhawaa'ikwe smiled. "We are not leaving here altogether, my little son."

~ ~ ~

In the days before they left, my grandparents and Wazhushk visited each of the four seasonal camps that had been the pattern of their lives, beginning with the wild rice camp on the shore of Lost Lake, which was just a short walk from the board house, because they had been there the most recently. From the rice camp they took only the cast-iron kettle, which Little Muskrat lifted from where it hung by a hook over the parching fire; he then pulled the hook down from the wooden stand he had made. The kettle and hook they would take because both, carried from Canada by Big Muskrat's own father, were precious. At the winter camp, which was farther away, a half day's walk beyond the rise, they dug for the traps they had wrapped in hides and cached under a stand of sumac; those they would need to continue their cash money and trading livelihood. From the maple sugar camp, the closest of all four camps to the house, Little Muskrat decided to take only the large wooden sugaring trough and leave anything else for the LaForces. Among the maples they searched once more for my great-grandmother's wooden maple sugar candy mold, that small, hand-sized trough with three stars carved into the bottom by Little Muskrat two winters before, not long before she died. Wazhushk had liked to press some of the last of the late spring snow, found only in shade by the time maple sugaring was over, into the mold, creating a hard, star-topped mound of ice over which his grandmother would pour maple syrup, a sweet delicacy loved by the little boy. At the end of sugaring two springs ago, he had wrapped the mold and set it next to the large wooden sugar-making trough, which Little Muskrat had turned upside down and covered. The next spring when Wazhushk looked for the mold, it had disappeared, and he had felt again the loss of his grandmother. In this last visit to the sugarbush, searching among dead leaves and brush for the outline of a small child-sized trough, for a glimpse of three six-pointed stars, his chest and throat ached with held-back tears.

"Ho! *Wazhushk, ambe oma! Waabindan!* Look what is here!" Little Muskrat in turning the sugaring trough over had found the candy mold wrapped carefully and placed not next to it, as the boy had thought he remembered, but beneath.

The boy unwrapped the package and fingered the stars, his feeling of loss sweetened by the candy mold and memory of his grandmother in the same way that the little candy mold was sweetened by the memory of maple sugar. He placed the mold carefully into the folds of the wool sash that he wore wound several times around his waist.

Little Muskrat stroked his son's hair. "Mino abinooji, giin," he said. "You are a good boy."

The summering camp was on the other side of the lake. There was nothing stored there that would be taken; on the way to the river bank they would stop there just to sit for a while at Wazhushk's favorite place, the outcropping of stone smooth and even as a floor, large enough for six or eight people to sit on while they fished. The summering camp was shared by several families and was a gathering place for social activity during the days of warmth and light. They would be back, Little Muskrat said. They would join the other families in early summer and stay through ricing, just before fall.

～ ～ ～

The new house by the Miskwaa River bank was built by Little Muskrat and Joseph with boards and nails provided by the government, a one-room tar-papered shack with one window, a wooden floor, a stoop, and a door. When Joseph reached adulthood and married, he brought to the house his wife, Liza, and that is where I, Zho Wash, was born in the late afternoon on a foggy day just as the sun began to shine through mist, turning the wall of white cloud outside the window into glowing silver for just a brief time.

My Zhaaganaashig name was Joseph Washington, like my father's; at home I was called Zho-zens, Little Joseph.

Our life was uneventful until when I was five years old my existence was discovered by Mr. Oliver, who sent me away from home to the Harrod Indian school, where one of the first things I was told to do was to use my English name, Joseph Washington. At first, I knew that this would never be; however, during my fourth beating at the hands of the school handyman, Mr. McGoun, I reconciled myself to it.

My parents died young, as many Indian people did and still do today; the winter I was fifteen they disappeared while walking along the riverbank on their way to Odanang, to trade their bundled pelts for coffee, flour, and a length of wool (my mother, Liza, was hoping that perhaps they might also bring home a small, gilt-framed mirror). Because they lived alone and a distance from Odanang and the Mozhay reservation allotments, their absence was not noticed by anyone for some time. On a windy day when the air tasted ever so slightly of warmer days to come and of sap beginning to stir in the trees, one of the Dionne brothers who was out checking his illegal traplines along the Miskwaa saw what looked like a large crow in distress atop a snowbank. The crow flapped its wings without calling; its dark body rose and fell, anchored by the feet to the snow. Antoine Dionne had never seen anything like that. Should he try to free it, he wondered, or might he have to kill it and end its suffering? He lay on his stomach back of a large drift and cautiously crawled closer to see; when the crow didn't appear to notice, he stood and walked to the body, which he saw then was not a crow but a length of dark green and black plaid wool, a lady's shawl, he saw when he pulled on it, frozen into an ice-crusted snowbank. Whose? Whose could it be? Might there be more? He lay on the bank and dug with his hands, found a small skin bag of frozen jerky, a crushed and empty willow basket, and then a red velvet cap that he recognized as Joseph Washington's, made by his mother-in-law, who was a cousin to Antoine. As he held the hat, brushing and shaking ice and snow from its folds, the wind picked up and the taste of warm days to come and sap beginning to stir in the trees disappeared; he realized that he felt chilled. His fingers and the palms of his hands were smeared with red dye from the hat, he saw. Wiping his nose on the back of his hand he smelled a rotting sweetness that he recognized as death. Were the smears not red dye? Could they be blood? Whose blood? Horrified, he dropped the shawl, skin bag, basket, and cap, and ran. He returned the next day with his brothers, who carried a kettle of lard that they lit a fire beneath as soon as they reached the spot. If a Windigo had attacked Joseph and Liza, it might return in hope of finding other humans to feast on. If that should happen, the men would have to try to kill it in the only way that a Windigo could be killed, by pouring boiling lard down its ravenous throat. As the older men built the fire, those with younger eyes looked in all directions for the tall and terrible figure with bits of raw human flesh stuck in its teeth and bloodstains on its cold yellow chest. Antoine, the most frightened of them all, shook like a dead birch branch in the wind.

No Windigo was seen; no Windigo approached. And there was no sign of Joseph's cap, Liza's shawl, the skin bag of dried venison that they would have eaten on their way to Odanang, or the crushed and empty willow basket.

The school superintendent told me that my parents had likely slipped from the riverbank and drowned in the Miskwaa, just above the rapids, where their bodies had probably been destroyed. Because I was now an orphan, I was to become a ward of the state, under the guardianship of the new Indian agent, Mr. Benson, who had replaced Mr. Oliver. Mr. Benson decided that I would remain at Harrod until the end of summer, when I would take a train to Lawrence, Kansas, where if I showed promise I might study in Haskell Indian School's commercial business program.

After I finished the program at Haskell, I didn't have any reason to return to Mozhay. After all, I was an orphan, an unallotted Indian who lived elsewhere, *aandakii*. I got a job as a clerk in a freight warehouse in Kansas City, close enough to visit the girl who had become my sweetheart.

Her name was Genevieve; I called her Eva. While at school she had developed a cough and so had been sent away to the state tuberculosis sanitarium until she was cured. Tuberculosis wrenched the breath and life from many Indians in those days; however, my Eva continued to breathe: I could hear it and also the deepening retch of her cough on Sunday afternoons as we waved and nodded to each other through the gauze screen that separated the sick from the well in the visiting room.

We were married by a justice of the peace in the visiting room, with a nurse on Eva's side of the gauze and a janitor on mine, for witnesses. After that a gauze curtain was hung in her room between her bed and the doorway and I was allowed to visit and talk from the other size of the gauze, seated on a white-painted wooden chair brought in for me by the nurse.

I don't know if anyone told my wife what the doctor had told me: that our marriage was not legal, that the justice of the peace would never file the papers, that it would never be consummated, that she would never leave the sanitarium. We never talked about that. Instead, I told her about the deep northern woods, the house by the Miskwaa River and the iciness of the rapids. *We'll go there when you are better,* I told her. *It is pretty there, cold and snowy in the winter; in early spring the air feels warm for maple sugaring; in late summer we feel the last of the heat during wild ricing. We'll go there when you are better,* I told my wife. *I am feeling stronger,* she told me, *stronger every day. Today I walked outside on the screened porch,* and did I imagine it, I wondered, were her eyes not shining, her cheeks rosy? *Was she getting better?* I asked the nurse, who shook her head. *It is the tuberculosis,* she said; *sometimes it looks like that as it progresses,* and the next Sunday I could see that my wife's eyes didn't shine so much as glitter, that her dry cheeks were not rosy so much as fever-burned.

I began to dream of my father's birthplace, the maple sugaring camp on the land that became the LaForce allotment. The first night I dreamed of maple trees in early spring, not yet leaved, yet beginning to regain their limberness as the cold winds of winter receded. Their branches waved in air warmed by longer days and the larger sun; sap began to rise, bringing a blush to the bark, then from crescents nicked into the tree trunks to drip, then flow slowly and steadily along carved shallow wooden troughs that had been inserted into the crescents, down to pitch-lined birch-bark baskets that had been set on the ground. The second night a man and woman gathered the small birch-bark baskets as they filled with sap and poured them into an iron kettle, where the sap steamed, sweetening the sky and the earth as it boiled down. I watched them work while the sap thickened; I watched the man tip the kettle into a large wooden trough, where he turned and kneaded the cooling mass, granulating into maple sugar. The third night the couple was joined by an old woman who held in one hand a small wooden bowl that had carved into the bottom three six-pointed stars; her other hand held the hand of a small boy, who she led to a snowbank. She scooped and packed snow into the bowl; the little boy brought it to his mother, who with a wooden spoon ladled over the snow sticky syrup from the batch the man was pouring into the trough. The couple and the old woman smiled to see the boy's pleasure as he ate the treat.

I told Eva of the dreams the next day, which was a Sunday,

the day the warehouse was closed. She lay in bed, across the room; through the white gauze visiting panel I saw her smile and could smile in return; through the panel of gauze her eyes were less bright, her cheeks less red, her beauty less frightening. The dreams were a gift, she thought, from my parents. I told her that when she got better we would go north, to the birthplace of my father. It would be our home, I told her. We would be home.

She asked me to tell her again about maple sugaring. When I got to the pouring of warm syrup over cold snow, she said, "When we have a son, we will smile that same way, to see his pleasure when he tastes that sweetness."

That night I didn't dream because she was so ill that I couldn't sleep, and during the next several weeks I slept for only short periods, when I couldn't stay conscious any longer and fell into stifling darkness. I would wake with a shock, sitting up and gasping to fill my lungs, to force air down the closed dryness of my throat and chest. Each time I thought that it was her death that woke me, the weight of her hand on my chest as she grasped to stay with the living. These terrors helped to prepare me for what was of course inevitable.

Her death occurred finally not with a sound but with the absence of sound when she simply stopped breathing on the other side of the gauze, in the darkness of her room. I listened for another inhalation, touched my ear and my hands to the wall of gauze that caught on my ink-stained fingertips that were roughened by their constant contact with paper and grit eraser. I inhaled for her, held my breath listening; when I exhaled my breath rippled the curtain. A nurse walked past the door and saw me; she donned a robe and mask that she took down from a hook outside the door, lifted the curtain at one side, and stepped inside. "You must step back," she said firmly.

I was not permitted inside the room, as her body was as infectious in death as it had been in life. The silence of her leaving was almost immediately filled by a muted roaring and moaning in my ears that rose and fell like a distant wolf in winter.

She was buried by the county. I have never visited there.

After, I slept dreamless every night, hungry for the taste and smell of oblivion, of nothingness that had become sweet when compared to the day, with its odors of brine and decay. Ah, blackness, I would think, and dive into its murkiness as the hero Wazhushk, the great and courageous Muskrat, had dived into the unknown vastness of the Great Flood to save us all. My dive into blackness, however, was not from selflessness and courage but the opposite: with night came the seductive possibility of death during sleep. I wondered if that was the sound I heard, the keening wolf in winter wailing mutely for my company.

One night the blackness opened to the fourth dream. It was autumn in the sugarbush; maple trees were beginning to drop red and yellow leaves to the ground. The mother and little boy entered the maple stand by themselves. With her hand she rubbed his back in circles, between his shoulder blades, in the same rhythm as the howl, which died as she spoke.

"Here is the secret I promised you, son. Before you were born, Wazhushk, your grandmother sewed you a little bag of deerskin embroidered with red thread and blue beads. This bag was for your odissimaa, that small stem left from the cord that connected you to your mother before you were born. When you were only a few days old the stem had dried and fallen from your little belly; your grandmother wrapped it in cattail fluff and placed it into the bag. Your father then buried the bag here in the maple sugar camp, sixteen long steps away from the kettle toward the sunrise. It has been here ever since, during the ten seasons of maple sugaring since you were born, and it will be here for a very long time, perhaps forever. So, do you see? Part of you is here, where someone else is going to live but where you were born and where we have lived. No matter where you go, your odissimaa will stay here, and because of that we will always be a part of this place. Don't cry, now; just remember this, and remember to come back again sometime to this place. You will want to do that."

~ ~ ~

I returned to Mozhay and to the place of my father's birth for my young wife and for him, and have many, many times walked over the place where his odissimaa, the cord that tied him from before birth to his mother, Ozhawaa'ikwe, and through her to the earth, is buried. Because of them the Muskrats are bound eternally and blessedly to the land that became the LaForce allotment: when my little Margie-enjiss gave birth to our daughter, Crystal, I asked her aunt Beryl to also keep her odissimaa close to her ancestors; when Crystal's baby is born, Margie will ask someone in whom she has great trust to do the same.

I believe that this could be the day that I will join my parents and grandparents and the Muskrat spirits who continue to watch over and bless the LaForce allotment. I will see our grandson before Margie does; with my death I will leave a place in this world for him. When he is born Crystal will watch as the doctor lays the baby limp and gray across her stomach; she will watch as he calmly draws in a slow and deep breath that pulls into his lungs the oxygen that will light his skin to gray-lavender, to lavender, to lavender-pink, to pink; her eyes will be met by her son's, dark and open as the lake on an overcast early winter afternoon; and the shell that has held and protected her heart will break with happiness too large to contain the self she was before that minute. She will watch the doctor perform the final physical separation of that new life from herself by cutting the umbilical cord, and will feel her first grief as a mother when the end of the cord that is attached to her son, his odissimaa, is clamped and he becomes a person physically separate from herself. When the dried stem of the odissimaa falls from his navel and she finds it loose in his quilt, she will give it to Margie who as *Nokomis*, Grandmother, will place it in the small deer-hide bag beaded with a turtle and knotted vines by her friend Theresa.

My own odissimaa was carried by my father, Joseph, in a bag sewn by my mother, Liza, of dark blue wool that had been the pocket of her skirt. The bag was the size of a small egg and embroidered with white thread in the curling shapes of wild grape tendrils. He wore it at his side, tied to his belt. I suppose that it disappeared into the Miskwaa Rapids with him, if that is where his body was indeed destroyed, or perhaps it was dropped by a Windigo just before it devoured my parents on the banks of the Miskwaa River just above the rapids, where it would have disappeared into the snow and melted against the ground during the thaw. *Maagizhaa;* perhaps the Dionnes walked around it or even on it during a covert check of their illegal traplines, the bag that held my odissimaa obscured by morning fog or the darkness of a night without a moon, just as they were obscured from the sight of the LaForces. *Maagizhaa;* perhaps a muskrat found it and dragged it to the muddy cave where its babies nested, to be smelled and played with and gnawed. *Maagizhaa;* perhaps it was found while I was still a boy by a lumberjack, or during the Depression by someone from the CCC camp nearby, or perhaps yesterday by a hiker in Gore-Tex with a bottle of Gatorade and a bag of gorp in his backpack. *Magizhaa;* perhaps it is still where it was dropped, covered by years of sumac spread, leaves of summer green and fall red; it could be part of the decay of leaves and dirt underneath the trunk of a fallen birch tree. *Amanj*, I don't know; *gaye, minawaa amanjidash*, and again I wonder.

When Ojibwe die, even the *Aandakii* Ojibwe who live elsewhere, our spirits walk to the next world through four days of trials and travails: this I have been told and have told others, as well as the end of the story that is also the beginning, which is that the dead are, at the same time as they are in heaven, always among the living. At the conclusion of my walk west it will be that way for me, too.

Magizhaa; perhaps as my spirit wanders from time to time over the lands of Mozhay Point it will softly brush the rocks by the Miskwaa River, or light as air skim the cold mightiness of the rapids. Perhaps my spirit will solemnly dance on the work-smoothed clearing of the sugarbush on the land that became the LaForce allotment, where it will come across the place where a deerskin bag hand-worked by my great-grandmother lies today. *Maagizhaa.*

The door opens softly; at the sound I open my eyes to the sight of Crystal, who stands in the doorway, fingers laced across the top of her stomach. Together we watch Margie dream, *nindaaniss dash niin,* as stars fade into a slowly brightening sky.

Then Crystal sits on the floor next to the bed and leans her head against the mattress. My hand resting on her soft hair, I begin in my old man's whisper to recount the story as in my daughter's eyes the Anishinaabe ancestors listen and nod *mii gwayak.*

Linda LeGarde Grover, a member of the Bois Forte Band of Ojibwe, is associate professor of American Indian studies at the University of Minnesota Duluth. *The Road Back to Sweetgrass* has been awarded the Native Writers' Circle of the Americas First Book prize. Grover's short-story collection *The Dance Boots* received the Flannery O'Connor Award for Short Fiction as well as the Janet Heidinger Kafka Prize.